CLB 7/H/10

MAR 6 1986

The *LAST*
UNION SOLDIER

*First-Sergeant Daniel Timothy Gallagher,
Provisional Company "A," First
United States Dragoons,*
was the last Union soldier in the Arizona Union outpost. Typhoid and Apaches had killed most; the few remaining were prisoners of the Confederacy.

Gallagher's orders from his dead captain were to ride into the Indian-infested Arizona Territory, recover a cache of ammunition, and hunt down the murderous gun-runner who planned to sell the stolen weapons to the Confederacy. The advancing Rebel troops counted heavily on the hidden cache; with it they would put the whole Pacific coast under the Confederate flag.

It was up to Gallagher—to save his captain's lovely daughter from the woman-hungry Apaches, to ride down Chief Yellow Snake and the outlaw Elijah Darris, to stop the Rebel drive. It was up to one courageous soldier to save himself, the woman he loved ... and the Union!

More Westerns from SIGNET

☐ **LAST TRAIN FROM GUN HILL by Gordon D. Shirreffs.** He had twelve hours to capture the man who had raped and murdered his wife.
(#Q6517—95¢)

☐ **MAN WITHOUT A GUN by Ray Hogan.** Slater had only his wits and fists to protect him as he fought to bring the ruthless killers to justice. . . .
(#Q6647—95¢)

☐ **LYNCHING AT BROKEN BUTTE by Lewis B. Patten.** What was the guilty secret the whole town tried to hide? A scorching new story of the West by the Spur Award-winning author.
(#Q6550—95¢)

☐ **TERROR IN EAGLE BASIN by Cliff Farrell.** Once the deadliest of lawmen, he'd turned his back on violence . . . but now he was forced to buckle on his guns again. (#Q6469—95¢)

☐ **THE LAST COMANCHERO by Ray Hogan.** Deep in the desert, Shawn Starbuck plays cat and mouse with the man who holds his brother captive—Valdez, leader of the Comancheros!
(#Q6426—95¢)

☐ **BOUNTY MAN by Lewis B. Patten.** Tracking down two desperate murderers, Ross Dunbar stops on a mission of mercy and finds himself trapped instead! (#Q6366—95¢)

THE NEW AMERICAN LIBRARY, INC.,
P.O. Box 999, Bergenfield, New Jersey 07621

Please send me the SIGNET BOOKS I have checked above. I am enclosing $_____(check or money order—no currency or C.O.D.s). Please include the list price plus 25¢ a copy to cover handling and mailing costs. (Prices and numbers are subject to change without notice.)

Name_____

Address_____

City_____State_____Zip Code_____

Allow at least 3 weeks for delivery

The BORDER GUIDON

BY

Gorden D. Shirreffs

A SIGNET BOOK
NEW AMERICAN LIBRARY
TIMES MIRROR

COPYRIGHT © 1962 BY GORDON D. SHIRREFFS

All rights reserved

SIGNET TRADEMARK REG. U.S. PAT. OFF. AND FOREIGN COUNTRIES
REGISTERED TRADEMARK—MARCA REGISTRADA
HECHO EN CHICAGO, U.S.A.

SIGNET, SIGNET CLASSICS, MENTOR, PLUME AND MERIDIAN BOOKS
are published by The New American Library, Inc.,
1301 Avenue of the Americas, New York, New York 10019

FIRST PRINTING, MARCH, 1963

2 3 4 5 6 7 8 9 10 11

PRINTED IN THE UNITED STATES OF AMERICA

Chapter 1

THE BITTER January wind swept across the parade ground of Fort McComber, slashing tiny pebbles and grit against the drab post buildings and rattling the flagpole halyards in mad frenzy against the tall warped pole. The flag streamed tautly in the wind, as hard as a sheet of metal, while the outer third of it was whipping itself into bright rags.

First Sergeant Daniel Timothy Gallagher, Provisional Company A, First United States Dragoons, left his quarters and braced himself against the battering of the wind as he fought his way across the *caliche* of the parade ground, wincing as pebbles stung his mahogany-hued face. The wind was howling in its insane triumph, and the sound of it was enough to make an Irishman think uncomfortably of banshees.

He struggled under the sagging ramada that shaded the officers' quarters when the molten Arizona sun beat down upon the isolated fort. Maybe the banshee *would* howl that very night, he thought, for death itself hovered in the officers' quarters of Fort McComber.

He fumbled for the handle, opened the door, and was propelled into the hallway by a wild gust of wind. He closed the door and placed his broad back against it. His eyes and nose were full of grit—even his thick reddish dragoon mustache was caked with it. Above the dry astringent odor of the desert wind he could smell the mingled odors of carbolic and sweat, sour vomit, and the sickly odor of approaching death.

Gallagher slowly passed his hands down his shell jacket and trousers to free them of dust. The orange dragoon stripes on his trousers were faded and threadbare—there had been no issue of new clothing since the war had begun somewhere in South Carolina, at a city named Charleston, at a fort named Sumter. That had been ten months ago, and it seemed as though the United States had quite forgotten isolated Fort McComber in Arizona and the handful of men who formed Provisional Company A.

A door opened slowly, emitting a flickering glow of yellow light, and the miasma in the hallway seemed to become thicker. The thin yellowish face of Medical Orderly Olney Little stared at Gallagher.

"Well," said Gallagher.

"It's worse than I thought, Sergeant."

"Get on with it, man!"

Little passed a hand across his sweating face. "It's typhoid, Sergeant."

A cold hand seemed to pass down Gallagher's spine. "Ye're sure?"

The orderly nodded. "The captain has all the symptoms: rising temperature, nausea, loss of appetite, headache, and nosebleed. Pains in the back and limbs. Pink spots on the abdomen."

"Could it be something else?"

Little's washed-out grey eyes blinked. "No."

"Ye are not a doctor, Little."

The man seemed to grow in stature. "I was . . . once," he said quietly.

"Ah!"

The orderly nodded. "You'd never have medical orderlies or company clerks in the Army if doctors and educated men didn't drink, Sergeant."

Gallagher nodded. "What happens now?" he asked with a new respect for the failure who stood before him.

Little passed a hand across his forehead again. Bright beads of sweat stood out on his sallow skin. "The symptoms usually appear from eight days to two weeks after infection. During the third week the fever begins to drop and the patient suffers from weakness, tremors of the muscles, delirium, and weak heart. This is the dangerous stage, Sergeant."

Gallagher added rapidly in his head. The commanding officer had come down with the sickness the second week in January, and now the month was drawing to a close. "Now," he said quietly.

"Yes."

"Is there any chance?"

"He is not a young man, Sergeant."

Gallagher nodded. He ground a big freckled fist into the palm of his other hand and listened to the wild wind scrabbling at the walls and roof of the quarters. Suddenly his hair seemed to rise at the nape of his neck as he heard an eerie moaning sound in a minor key below the roaring threnody of the wind.

Little smiled whimsically. "It is not the banshee, Sergeant Gallagher. It is the captain."

"Can I go in?"

The orderly passed a hand across his forehead again. "It is highly infectious."

"The breath? I will stay far back."

"Not the breath. The body discharges are said to carry the disease."

"Ye do not look well, Little," said Gallagher, eying the orderly closely.

"I have been on duty for twenty-four hours."

"They did not think enough of us at headquarters to allow us a surgeon," said Gallagher bitterly. He walked into the sick room, and the aura in it was enough to make his strong stomach moil within him.

Captain, Brevet Colonel, D'Arcy Hastings Eustis, lay flat on his back, looking up at the fly-specked ceiling with wide eyes that did not seem to see. His thin hands plucked steadily at the sweat-damp sheet—the skin on them seemed like that of a freshly plucked chicken. They were hands that once could swing a heavy issue Chicopee saber easily in left and right moulinets, thrusts, and slashes. Now they could not snap a match. The officer's classic face seemed etched in marble, and the fine thin nose stood out from the sunken face like that of a Roman bas-relief.

How old was he? thought Gallagher. He looked over sixty. Gallagher had ridden with him for almost ten years, from private up through the grades to first soldier, from Texas to New Mexico, from New Mexico to Utah, from Utah to California, and back again to New Mexico. There was no better Indian-fighter on the wide frontier where a handful of men in blue held off thousands of hostiles and taught them respect for cavalry, mounted rifles, and dragoons, with the emphasis on the last.

The room reflected the personality and character of D'Arcy Hastings Eustis. His fine Castellani saber hung over the beehive fireplace. A cased pair of dueling pistols lay on the chipped marble-topped table beside the bed, and ranks of medicine bottles, glasses, and spoons surrounded the morocco leather case. There were a number of fine pencil drawings hanging on the walls. Gallagher knew every one of them for he had often seen the captain sketching on his pad, even as he rode through the Big Country. The drawings on the walls were almost a history of the captain and his company of dragoons. His violin was in its case and on its shelf; many a night the officer had played for his men about the campfires in mountains or desert, with the soft music vying with that of the whispering wind and the muted howling of the coyotes.

The officer moved a little and looked at Gallagher, but the big noncom had the impression that Captain Eustis was looking right through him to something that could be seen only by a man who was waiting for the Angel of Death. Then Captain Eustis sang softly in his fine voice:

"Oh, the dragoon bold! He scorns all care,
As he goes the rounds with uncropped hair;
He spends no thought on the evil star
That sent him away to the border war."

Many a time had Gallagher heard the officer sing that song. Every time the going got rough and the chips were down he would sing that old ballad in defiance of fate.

Gallagher wiped the sweat from his face. It was stifling hot in the little room.

"I won't keep you long, Gallagher," said the officer quietly.

"There is no hurry, sir."

The officer shook his head. "But there *is*." His voice trailed off. He turned his head a little and then placed a thin hand on his forehead.

"The dispatches have not come in yet this week, sir," said Gallagher. He hated to tell the old man that, for the captain had been waiting months for orders to leave Fort McComber and join the rest of the Army, wherever the fighting was thickest against the rebels. Gallagher had it in his mind that D'Arcy Eustis would be up and about if those orders had come. Had they forgotten the old man after all these years of service to his country?

Eustis nodded. "Where is Mister Artenis?"

"In his quarters, sir. He is not feeling well." Why tell the old man his second-in-command was filthy drunk and had been so for days?

"And young Mister Tyrel?"

"He has gone out with a detachment to look for the courier from New Mexico, sir."

Eustis nodded. "A good soldier, that boy. Not a dragoon as yet, but a good soldier. He will do well." The gray eyes twinkled. "When I am gone it will be Sergeant Dan Gallagher who will forge him into the fine Damascus steel of a real dragoon."

Gallagher reddened. "Ah, sir!"

The eyes closed. "Let me see the dispatches when they arrive. I want to sleep now."

Gallagher saluted and spun about. He walked into the dim hallway. The orderly lay flat on his face near the outer door. Gallagher knelt beside him and rolled him over. He placed a big rough hand on the yellowish forehead and swore softly. The little man was burning up with fever. There was a trickle of blood coming from his nostrils. Gallagher unbuttoned the man's shell jacket, pulled up his thick woolen undershirt. The thin belly was stippled with faint pinkish spots. "For the love av Heaven," breathed Gallagher.

He carried the little man into an empty room and covered him with several blankets. Gallagher shoved back his forage cap and eyed Little. It was typhoid, sure enough. It was what had frightened Mister Artenis into a three-day drunk and what had caused a shadow of fear and panic to hover over the isolated outpost. They all knew that something more than just a fever had attacked Captain Eustis.

As Gallagher walked outside the wind battered at him. It was a hell of a place, this Fort McComber, a fort in name only in southern Arizona, surrounded by great hairless mountains, dull leaden in color, that seemed to brood over the vast desolation below them. The place was out on the Devil's hind limb and had only one reason for its existence—it kept the Tonto and Chiricahua Apaches from sweeping the hated white-eyes from that country. McComber did not protect the mines or the small towns that had been slowly springing up throughout the territory since the Mexican War. McComber was there to keep the travel routes open by the use of its long arm of forty hard-pratted dragoons. The duty had developed into an almost personal feud between Klij-Litzogue—Yellow Snake, predatory war leader of the Tontos—and First Sergeant Dan Gallagher. The odds were about even on them.

But now that the war was on there seemed little reason for McComber's occupation. In the past six months frontier post after frontier post had been abandoned, stripped of their garrisons of regulars who were needed in Virginia, Tennessee, and New Mexico. Indeed, most of the First Dragoons were in another theater of war, and Company A was with the regiment. It had been a belly blow to the old man who had commanded Company A for so many years when he found out that the company designation had been given to a newly formed unit, to keep the regiment up to full fighting strength, while his company, *the* Company A, had been redesignated as a "provisional" company. But they still had their old guidon despite the fact that some company calling itself A was riding with the regiment. As far as Captain Eustis and First Sergeant Gallagher were concerned the dragoons garrisoning forgotten Fort McComber were Company A, First Dragoons.

"They've forgotten we exist," said Gallagher bitterly.

He walked toward the guardhouse and kicked open the warped door in his cold anger.

"Jesus!" said Corporal Hallahan, "do ye have to kick down yon door, Dan?"

"Shut yer gob! Have ye seen any sight of Mister Tyrel?"

"Divil a one, Dan."

Gallagher shook his head. Tyrel had the makings of a good dragoon, but he was young, impetuous and hungry for glory, and such men were fair game for Yellow Snake. He played a waiting game. He had the time and the patience, and the country fought for him better than it did for the white soldiers.

"He has been gone a long time," said Private Henry.

"Aye," said Hallahan.

Gallagher nodded. The young shavetail had but ten men with him, and one skilled noncom, Corporal Heinrich —hardly enough for a fight with the Tontos. They had become increasingly bold of late. *They knew*. They had seen post after post abandoned. They had seen the funeral pyres of stores, blankets, medicines, saddles, tents, spare uniforms and all the other impedimenta of an established garrison rising above the empty barracks and buildings. Post after post, like beads widely spaced on a thin string, had been abandoned, and the Apaches had swept in again to the country where they had fought with, and been defeated by, the men in blue. Chiricahuas, Warm Springs, White Mountain, Mohave Apaches, Jicarillas, and the ultrapredatory Tontos had come into their own again. Gallagher had it in his mind that they were laughing silently at Fort McComber and its pitiful garrison of a handful of slowly demoralizing dragoons.

"Why are we left here in this outpost of hell?" growled Private Kitridge. "The rest of the regiment is gone. The whole damned territory, from the Colorado right clear to the Rio Grande, hasn't a garrisoned post in it except for Fort McComber."

"True," said Hallahan sourly.

There was no use in telling them to shut up. They were right. Forts Buchanan, Breckenridge, McLane, and Mohave had been abandoned. Arizona was now the bloody playground of Apache, Paiute, Mohave and Navajo. Between Fort Yuma, on the California side of the Colorado River, and possibly Fort Craig, on the northern Rio Grande in New Mexico Territory—somewhere between four hundred and four hundred and fifty miles—there were no United States troops to hold the hostiles in check or to prevent the Confederates taking over the whole kit and caboodle. Latrine rumors had it that the rebels already were invading New Mexico, and if they invaded New Mexico, Arizona would be next.

"Maybe they forgot we're here," said Private Henry.

"Yellow Snake hasn't," said Kitridge.

They all looked at each other.

"Go get my horse and saddle him," said Gallagher to Henry.

"You don't mean to tell me you're riding out there, Sergeant?"

"Don't ask questions! Get the bloody horse!"

"And ye go out and patrol the rounds," said Hallahan to Kitridge.

"In this wind? You're loco!"

One of Hallahan's big hands gripped the front of Kitridge's shell jacket and twisted it, pulling the big dragoon to his feet, and Hallahan's right fist smacked neatly against his jaw. "Git!" roared Hallahan.

The dragoon scuttled from the room. Gallagher impatiently walked outside to wait for Henry to bring him a horse. When the big bay came it seemed listless. Gallagher swung up into the McClellan and checked his Enfield musketoon. His Navy Colt was holstered at his side.

The wind lashed across the mesa top, sweeping tumbleweeds ahead of it. Some of them were banked high against the corrals, stables, and barracks. Vast whorls of yellowish dust hung against the dull sky. The rutted road to the east was hard to distinguish. Gallagher tied his orange scarf about his nose and mouth and hunched in his saddle. The wind muttered obscenely in his ears, and the foul thoughts it placed in his mind sickened him. He drove off the feeling of impending doom and disaster and rode on into the sweeping dust clouds, a big man, as hard as lignum vitae and spring steel.

Chapter 2

THE WIND died away as he descended the side of the mesa toward the dry watercourse that snaked along the foot of the elevation. He peered through irritated eyes toward the flatlands east of the watercourse. There was a movement out there, but it was hard to distinguish. In a little while he made out the dusty blue of uniforms. He grinned. Mister Tyrel had found the dispatch rider. Gallagher's fears had been for nothing.

He urged the bay on, but the big mount was strangely listless. Gallagher wiped the dust from his face and mustache. It was then that he saw the quick, almost indistinguishable movement on top of the low mounds that paralleled the road on each side. Coyotes perhaps? But they were rarely seen in the daytime and never that close to humans.

Gallagher stood up in his stirrups, wishing to God he had the captain's fine Vollmer field glasses.

Mister Tyrel was riding easily, with reins in his left hand and his right hand resting gracefully on his hip. Behind him clattered the escort. About half of them were greenies, fish, new rookies from the East, while the remainder, with the exception of hard-bitten Corporal Heinrich, had little experience in Indian-fighting other than scattered skirmishing.

Gallagher stared at those mounds and suddenly knew what was moving on them. Apaches! He stabbed the bay with his spurs and swung his clumsy Enfield musketoon forward and capped the nipple.

Mister Tyrel saw Gallagher and waved at him.

Gallagher thrust his Enfield toward the mounds and yelled at the top of his voice. It was too late. The dull-colored heaps of earth and ragged brush sprouted orange-red blossoms, and half of the escort went down on the dusty road. A horse reared and threw its rider. Another took the bit in its mouth and raced back the way the party had come, but a lead slug was faster than the horse, and its rider died with a bullet in his back.

Tyrel freed his saber and Colt and tried to rally his men, but it was no use. They broke for the open road. Instantly half-naked figures, crouched low on ponies, lanced out of the thick brush and cut in from both sides, like the horns of a crescent.

"Don't run, for God's sake!" bellowed Gallagher. "Stand! Stand and fight man to man! They cannot stand that!"

But it was no use. Panic had saddled up and now rode stirrup to stirrup with the routed dragoons. Apaches closed in and rifles and pistols cracked at short range, like shooting fish in a barrel. Corporal Heinrich reared up in his saddle as a pipe-axe struck home through his forage cap fair into the top of his skull and blood and brains spurted against the fresh, sunburned face of Mister Tyrel.

"Stand and fight!" screamed Gallagher. Then he was into the melee like a madman. His Enfield cracked, and the slug drove into the chest of a screaming brave. He reversed the weapon, stood up in his stirrups, and brought the butt down hard on the skull of another buck, driving him to the ground. The stock shattered, but the barrel was still there, and it did yeoman work while the bay drove hard against the lighter Apache ponies, guided by Gallagher's strong thigh pressures.

The musketoon barrel slipped from his sweating grasp. He hurled it full into the face of a buck whose nose was smashed beneath the impact. The buck's eyes stared into Gallagher's like those of a demon peering from a smoky window of hell itself. There was no mistaking those eyes. It was Klij-Litzogue!

The fight broke like a bloody fistula on the flats. The bucks screamed in sheer ecstasy for the success of their ambush, but they were paying for their minor victory now—paying it out in cold hard cash to the screaming, battling Irishman who yelled insanely as he whipped out saber and Colt and went to his work like a butcher cutting meat. *"I've come to stày!"* he roared as he stood up in the stirrups and laid about himself with his bloody Chicopee saber.

The one man drove them back; the big man with the three orange stripes and diamond of a first soldier on the faded sleeves of his jacket. Finally, he sat his weary horse alone in the blood-spattered road. But Yellow Snake urged his warriors on. Mister Tyrel had been unhorsed, but he swung up on the back of another bay and spurred it toward Gallagher, through the milling warriors and past his dead and wounded escort, for none of them were on foot or horse by now.

They let him pass part of the way through, and then Yellow Snake, with blood masking his face, stood up in his leathern stirrups, drew a short mulberry wood bow back to his ear, and released the thick cane shaft. It struck Arnold Tyrel full in the breastbone and stayed there quivering as he rode toward Gallagher with nerveless hands still tangled in the reins.

As the officer passed him Gallagher prepared for an Apache charge, but nothing Yellow Snake could do would make those sullen bucks charge the redheaded madman sitting the big bay in the center of the road. Slowly they drew back. There was other, more enjoyable work to be done now. The mutilating of the dead after they had been stripped; the skull crushing of the dead and severely wounded; the binding of the lesser wounded for transport to Yellow Snake's hidden rancheria in the Diablos, where they would be delivered into the greasy hands of the squaws for their final work with knife and fire.

Gallagher turned the bay and rode slowly toward the distant figure of Mister Tyrel. The officer still sat his horse, and as Gallagher drew near he turned, smiled a little, then fell heavily from the saddle.

The yellow lamplight flickered steadily in the draft, casting shadows on the whitewashed walls of the little dispensary. Gallagher wiped the sweat from his face, gripped the scalpel and began to cut.

"Not too deep, Gallagher, for the love av God!" husked Hallahan in Gallagher's ear.

"Ye've been in the medical alcohol, ye scut," growled Gallagher.

"A man needs a drink, Dan!"

The blood ran down Gallagher's hands as he gripped the cane shaft and began to work it free from bone and flesh.

"Agghhhh!" screamed the officer.

Hallahan and Private Devito's hands held him down as he writhed in excruciating agony.

"Agghhhh!"

"For the love av God, Gallagher, hurry!" cried Hallahan.

" 'Tis out!"

He held the bloody flint arrowhead in his big reddened hands. "Close," he murmured. Then he stared closely at the arrow point. He turned, and dipped it into the pinkish water of the basin, and then rinsed it. He held the point close to the lamp, and his stomach turned over within him.

"What is it, Dan?" asked Hallahan in a low voice.

Gallagher looked at the officer. He was unconscious. "Poisoned arrow," said Gallagher quietly.

"Ye mean that?"

"Aye!" Gallagher held it close to Hallahan. "See the brown gummy stuff on the point?"

Hallahan nodded.

"They take the fresh liver av a deer and cast it upon a hill of great red Sonóran ants, and the ants fill it with their poison as they bite into it. Then the liver is dried and mixed with grease, and other foul substances for aught I know. They carry it in wee bags and daub it onto their arrow points. They can kill game with these points, and eating av the meat does not affect them."

"And a man's meat, Dan?"

"Gangrene, Mike."

"There is no hope?"

Gallagher looked at the white naked chest of the young officer, laced with coagulating streaks of blood. "In a limb we could halt it by amputation. What can we do with that wound?"

Devito finished bathing the deep wound with a strong carbolic solution and then placed a pad upon the wound. He bound it about the officer's body. He looked up at Gallagher. "Will you tell him, *Sargento?*"

Gallagher wiped his face. "I do not know."

"If it is gangrene he will know soon enough," said Hallahan. "The poor lad!"

Gallagher walked outside carrying the dispatch case he had found attached to Tyrel's saber belt. It was dark, and the wind was still moaning as it swept across the naked mesa and battered insensately at the fort as though to drive it from the mesa as it drove tumbleweeds helter-skelter miles and miles across the lonely country.

He looked to the east. None of Tyrel's men had come in. It was now hours after the fight, and Gallagher did not expect any of them. He strode over to the quarters that Lieutenant Millard Artenis shared with Mister Tyrel. He opened the outer door and stepped into the hallway that divided the two rooms of the building. The left-hand doorway showed a thin line of yellow light beneath it. Gallagher tapped on the door with a big hand. There was no answer. He tapped harder. Still no answer. "Mister Artenis!" he called out.

It was quiet in the room; it was *too* quiet.

"Mister Artenis!"

There was a faint rustling noise within.

"Mister Artenis!" Gallagher almost added, *"Dammit, sir!"*

He waited a few minutes and then opened the door. The stench that flowed out was enough to sicken a man who had come from the wind-swept atmosphere outside. Sour liquor slops and sweat intermingled with other odors.

A candle guttered in the neck of a bottle and the light glistened on a set of Spanish half-armor and a morion helmet that hung on one wall. Mister Artenis had found it deep in a canyon of the Daiblos while on patrol and had removed the dried bones from within and given them Christian burial in the post cemetery. Gallagher had wondered at the time how long that spider-infested armor had been lying there in the loneliness, saved from rusting destruction by the dry air.

The officer sat on his rumpled bed with his back straight against the wall and his hands flat on the coverlet at each side of his hips. His brown eyes stared straight ahead of him fixedly. His thin hair hung over his sweating forehead, and was pasted to it in a tangled pattern. He had on his long dragoon trousers and high shoes but was naked from the waist up; beads of pearly sweat worked down through the sparse black hair on his chest.

"Mister Artenis, sir!"

The brown eyes looked at Gallagher but they did not see him.

Gallagher looked about the room. The man had not been out of the quarters for several days, except perhaps to go to the sanitary sinks behind the quarters, but even so the room stank of urine and sweat. Several empty bottles lay on the floor. Another, half full, was on the table. Gallagher walked over to the table and looked down at the officer. "Mister Artenis?" he said.

"What do you want, Gallagher?"

"The captain is taken bad, sir. Mister Tyrel was wounded by Apaches while escorting the dispatch rider. We lost twelve men counting the dispatch rider. I have the dispatches here, sir."

Artenis wiped the sweat from his face. "Hand me the bottle," he said.

Gallagher resisted an impulse to pull the man to his feet and smash in his drunken face.

"You Irish sonofabitch, hand me the bottle," said Mister Artenis in a flat clear voice.

"Mister Artenis, the lieutenant is in command now and is the only officer left able to command." Gallagher glanced at the bottle. Typhoid had laid Eustis low, and an arrow had dropped Mister Tyrel, but that had been no fault of theirs, while this drunken scut lay in his quarters.

Artenis moved quickly. His left hand came up with a

cocked double-barreled derringer; the twin muzzles looked almighty big to Gallagher. "Hand me the bottle, Gallagher."

"Ye have to take command, sir!"

The brown eyes looked as hard and as unreasoning as the twin muzzles of the little gun with the big bite. *"The bottle."*

Gallagher shrugged. He picked up the bottle with his right hand and walked toward the bed.

The gun came up and centered on Gallagher's flat belly. "I ought to kill you, you Irish sonofabitch! You goddam loyal patriotic bastard!"

Gallagher stared at the man.

"Wear the blue, Irishman! Salute the Stars and Stripes! Do your duty to your adopted country!"

"I will that, sir," said Gallagher quietly.

"Do you know something? People like you are riffraff. The gutter sweepings of Europe."

"Aye," said Gallagher slowly, "call me names, sir. And ye lie here in a drunken wallow whilst the captain is dying and Mister Tyrel has nothing but long agony before he too dies as sure as fate."

"It's useless to talk to you."

Gallagher stepped back and placed the bottle on the table. "I feel the same way about ye, sir, beggin' yer pardon. But there is work to be done. This foreign filth, as ye call me, has his duty to do. The dispatches have come in. The captain is hardly capable av holding his command. Will ye take the dispatches, sir? For the last time, I'm asking ye?"

"And if I tell you to go to hell?"

The big Irishman turned ever so slowly. "I will take command here, sir."

Gallagher opened the door and stepped into the hallway. For a long moment ice-locked blue eyes clashed like tempered steel with the amber-hard eyes of the officer. Artenis at last turned away. "Get out of here," he said thinly.

Gallagher closed the door behind him. His great hands opened and closed, then he left the quarters and walked toward Captain Eustis' quarters. The wind raged across the lonely fort. There were long and deadly miles between it and any other fort still flying the flag of the United States. A cold, unholy feeling came over Gallagher, and there was a fleeting impulse within him to get his horse, some rations, and his weapons and grease out of there for Mexico or perhaps California, and to hell with his duty.

Chapter 3

OLNEY LITTLE was dead. His thin birdlike hands clutched the rough edges of the gray issue blankets, and his wide-open eyes stared up at the ceiling of the dark cold room. Although his face was drawn and sunken there was a look upon it almost of relief, for Olney Little, once a doctor of medicine, was through with the bottle and the world forever.

Gallagher drew the blankets up over the set face of the little man. He had never paid much attention to the medical orderly. The Regular Army had a good leavening of his type. Educated men who had jousted with the bottle and had been unhorsed time and time again until home, wives, children, friends and respect all vanished in an alcoholic haze.

Gallagher closed the door and walked across to the captain's room. Captain Eustis was awake. The candlelight postured and danced on the whitewashed walls. The case of fine dueling pistols had been opened, and the light glinted from the exquisite silver chased barrels and the ivory and ebony inlays of the graceful and slender butts. They were the officer's most prized possession next in importance to his violin. Gallagher had never known the old man to use them except for shooting at marks, and their accuracy matched their appearance.

Captain Eustis eyed Gallagher. "You seem to get bigger every year, Gallagher."

" 'Tis the fine Army food, sir."

Eustis smiled wanly. Then a slight spasm seized him. He fought for control. "You have the dispatches?"

"Aye, sir."

"Read the important ones to me. You can take care of the routine matters." Eustis indicated a chair. "Sit

THE BORDER GUIDON 23

down. We have been comrades too long to stand on formality."

Gallagher sat down at the table. Officer and non-com, gentleman and tough Irishman, they had been friends for ten years. Gallagher opened the case. There was a dark patch of blood on the cover. He turned the case so that the stain could not be seen by the officer. He riffled through the contents. Routine matters, most of them, pertaining to allotments, requisitions and other matters now of little importance. Gallagher mentioned each of them in turn and placed to one side at a wave of Eustis' thin hand.

There were two items left in the case: a sealed official letter and another smaller envelope. He opened the sealed letter first and looked up at the officer. Captain Eustis had dropped off into one of his comalike dozes. Gallagher eyed the address on the official envelope: Captain D'Arcy H. Eustis, Provisional Company A, First United States Cavalry, Fort McComber, Territory of New Mexico.

"Cavalry is it?" he said harshly. "Some stupid ass av a clerk at Fort Marcy does not know we are dragoons!"

He scanned through the dispatch and his face paled beneath the reddish tan of it. He looked up at the captain and then down at the dispatch once more. It was long-winded but the gist of it was that Fort McComber was the last occupied U. S. military post in Arizona, and Company A. was the last unit of the United States Regular Army still on duty there. Federal forces in New Mexico proper were expecting an attack by a column of Texas mounted rifles whose obvious objective was to advance north up the valley of the Rio Grande, defeat the Federal forces, occupy Albuquerque and Santa Fe, capture Fort Union with its vast supply of military stores and rally Southern sympathizers to the Confederate flag. Definite information from secret agents in Southern New Mexico indicated that a unit of Texas mounted rifles was already advancing west into Arizona, with the objective of capturing Tucson and, later, Fort Yuma, California, on the Colorado River. This was all part of a plan to conquer the West Coast for the Confederacy.

Information received by Federal officers in New Mexico had indicated that the column advancing into Arizona was not well equipped, but that they expected to find better arms and equipment *in* Arizona. A large store of military equipment—Sharps, breech-loading, carbines, Springfield muzzle-loading rifles, Colt revolving pistols, all with ammunition, as well as six brass mountain howitzers, with charges, projectiles, friction primers and all necessary accessories, had supposedly been shipped in November, 1861, from Fort Coulter to Fort Breckenridge, for transshipment to Fort Craig in New Mexico. The smaller supplies were immediately shipped to Fort Craig where they were stored until January, 1862, when they were opened and it was discovered that the cases contained only rocks and sand. There was no record of the brass howitzers ever having been received at Fort Breckenridge, nor had they ever arrived at Fort Craig.

This indicated either that the equipment and guns had been lost or destroyed by enemy agents or sympathizers or, what was infinitely worse, that they were hidden somewhere in the vicinity of Fort Coulter ready to be picked up by the rebel troops now thought to be advancing into Arizona. The possession and use of the guns and equipment by the enemy might very well tilt the scales in their favor in their intended invasion of California.

Gallagher read the last paragraph aloud in the quiet room.

"You will therefore immediately upon receipt of these orders destroy all untransportable government property at Fort McComber, render all facilities useless, blow up all post buildings, and abandon the area. You will then take your command, in its entirety, and institute an immediate and intensive search for the missing equipment in the vicinity of Fort Coulter, and either satisfy yourself *conclusively* that the cache has been destroyed, or destroy it yourself, if it is impossible to withdraw it from the area, to prevent capture by the enemy.

"Upon completion of this mission, you will take your command either to Fort Yuma, California, on the Colorado River, or to Fort Craig, New Mexico Territory, on

the Northern Rio Grande, to report for further duty . . ."
Gallagher's voice trailed off. The impact of the dispatch
had struck him like a dose of grape at point-blank range.
He knew Fort Coulter well enough. It was to the west,
across malpais country and through rough hills. A hard
journey on man and beast. There was something else, too.
Fort Coulter had been built in the Diablos for one reason,
and only one reason. It was in the very heart of the
country once fully dominated by Klij-Litzogue and his
predatory Tontos. Since the post had been abandoned in
the fall of 1861 Klij-Litzogue had again ruled that country
with bloody hands. *If he got his hands on those weapons
and munitions...*

But if the rebels got the weapons it would be far
worse. Then nothing could stop them in their sweep to
the Pacific Coast. It was likely they would advance west
via the Great Southern Overland Route, through La Mesilla, Apache Pass, Dragoon Springs and Tucson. That
gave the dragoons one advantage; they were closer to Fort
Coulter than the rebels were.

"Aye," said Gallagher bitterly. "Some advantage!
With a sick commanding officer, a drunken second-in-command, and a dying shavetail for officers while we
have nought but thirty-odd dragoons left on the post."
Not enough to hold the post; not, by a damn sight,
enough to force a march to Fort Coulter on an important
mission which might, in the long run, by a twist of
malicious fate have a definite effect on the final result of
the war itself.

Gallagher tugged at his thick mustache. Christ, but he
wanted to get back to the regiment, whether it was called
cavalry or dragoons or anything else, for that matter.
"First Cavalry," he said sourly. It would not rest well
with the old man, either.

Captain Eustis opened his eyes. "Well, Gallagher," he
said quietly.

Gallagher read the dispatch. The officer lay there for a
long time looking fixedly at the ceiling. "First Cavalry,"
he said in a remote voice. "For eighteen years we have
been the First Dragoons. It will be hard to remember

that we are now cavalry. At least we are the *First* Cavalry —that is as it should be."

"Your orders, sir?" asked Gallagher.

Another long pause. "They will be obeyed to the letter. We will take no wagons to Fort Coulter. Each man will carry forty rounds for the musketoon and twenty for the Colt revolving pistol. Issue any extra revolving pistols so that each man will have two, as far as the supply lasts. Extra ammunition will be carried by mules. Two hundred rounds reserve supply for musketoons. Fifty for the Colts."

Gallagher eyed the officer. His face was sheet white and drawn. It was hard to recognize him except for the great eyes.

"Mister Tyrel will be in charge of the destruction of government property and of the blowing up of the buildings. Mister Artenis will be in charge of the post until I am on my feet."

Gallagher stood up. It wasn't likely Captain Eustis would be out of his bed for many a day. Meanwhile those stores at Fort Coulter would perhaps be lost to the United States, either to Klij-Litzogue or to the rebels. There was little time to waste. Yet they could not leave the old man. And it was certain he could not travel, even in an ambulance, across that country.

Eustis looked at Gallagher. "I rely greatly upon you, Gallagher. Mister Artenis is a good officer, but he has his weaknesses."

Yes, sir," said Gallagher. *God yes!*

The wind moaned piteously about the quarters, and the candles guttered crazily in the searching draft.

Captain Eustis slowly sat up and looked directly at Gallagher. The big Irishman's skin crawled at the look on the officer's face. It was almost as though a man cold in death had suddenly sat up in his casket at a wake. "It may not be that I will lead the company to Fort Yuma or to Fort Craig, Sergeant. But I *will* lead them until I am no longer able to."

How long, oh God?

"This company is Company A of the First Dragoons,

no matter what Washington has decided to redesignate us. The company has been assigned a dangerous mission. Most likely a hopeless one, but we will obey those orders to the letter!"

To the last man, and there were hardly enough of them left to go around if Klij-Litzogue caught them on the march.

"The company, when it reports for duty, at whichever camp, post or station it reaches after the completion of its mission, will ride in *under the company guidon.* If there is *one* man left, and *one* only, *that man will return the guidon to the regiment,* Sergeant Gallagher!"

"Aye, sir!"

For a moment it almost seemed as though D'Arcy Hastings Eustis would get up from that sweat-soaked bed and stand ramrod erect as he always did when taking over the company from First Sergeant Daniel Gallagher after morning roll call.

" 'Tis impossible," breathed Gallagher.

"If there is *one* man left, and *one* only, *that man will return the guidon to the regiment,* Sergeant Gallagher!"

"Aye, sir."

The wide eyes held Gallagher's attention as though hypnotizing him. *"But only when the mission has been completed successfully,* Sergeant Gallagher!"

"Aye, sir."

Then the officer fell back. Gallagher waited. A chill seemed to creep into the room. The candle flames bowed and postured in some meaningless ritual of their own.

The man was very still, though his eyes were still open.

The wind brushed against the walls.

Gallagher stepped close to the bed. The officer did not move. Gallagher bent close to the dry lips. He placed a hand on the captain's forehead, then took up his left wrist and held it with a big finger on the pulse. He placed the hand gently beside the still body and then slowly drew the damp sheet up over the face.

Gallagher turned and snuffed out all but one candle. He closed the lid of the dueling-pistol case and picked up the dispatches to put them in the case. It was then that he remembered the smaller envelope in the case. He held it up to the candle and saw that it had been addressed to the captain in a fine handwriting, no doubt that of a woman. Penciled at the bottom of the envelope, in strong masculine handwriting, was the forwarding note. The letter had originally been addressed to Captain Eustis in care of Fort Marcy, Santa Fe. Gallagher replaced it in the case. It would have to be returned with the captain's effects to his next of kin. Odd that Gallagher had never heard the captain mention any "next of kin" in all the years they had known each other.

He walked to the door and opened it. He glanced back at the bed, then closed the door behind him. As he stepped out under the ramada he heard a mournful howling out on the mesa. A coyote. He walked toward headquarters. The howling came again, faintly and dismally, almost lost in the whining of the night wind. Gallagher stopped and listened, with the wind drying the sweat on his face. He had never heard a coyote that close to Fort McComber, but then it didn't sound quite like a coyote either. The pitch of the howl was different. He had heard a sound like that before somewhere.

It wasn't until he was in the dark headquarters, feeling for a candle lantern, that he remembered where he had heard that sound before. It had been in Ireland when his father had died during a cold winter night. His big hands fumbled as he lighted the candle. "Ah, Gallagher," he said thickly, forcing back the strange thoughts in his Irish mind, "there are no banshees. At least none in America."

The howling came softly once more, and then it was gone.

Chapter 4

THE WIND had died away by the time of the false dawn and the softly graying light flowed over the desert country and across the naked mesa to Fort McComber, last garrisoned outpost of the United States in the vast part of New Mexico Territory known as Arizona. There was a loneliness about the drab little collection of buildings, set in their straight rows and alignments, as though a meticulous child had been playing in that Godforsaken spot and then had been driven away by the brooding melancholy of the atmosphere.

Lonely and forbidding, there was nothing else to call it, thought Dan Gallagher as he walked toward the first of the two barracks buildings. He had been up all night going through the files, destroying material that could not be taken along; placing important papers—and there were few enough of those—in a dispatch box. He had written out a plan of destruction, and now it was time to get the garrison ready for their mission.

Mike Hallahan met him at the door of the barracks.

" 'Tis fine news I have for ye, Dan," he said quietly.

"So? I could use a bit of fine news." Dan shoved back his forage cap. "The old man is dead, Mike."

Hallahan nodded. "I knew it. The banshee was about last night."

"Bull crap!"

The corporal eyed Gallagher. "Ye know it was, Danny," he said wisely.

"Get on with yer news!"

Hallahan waved a hopeless hand. " 'Tis me platoon, Dan. Nine av them pulled out last night sometime betwixt tattoo and the first light av dawn. Kitridge was behint it. I know."

Gallagher stared at him as though stunned. "Ye mean it?"

"Aye! I was tired. I've been on a lot of fatigues, Dan, as ye well know, what with the shortage of trained noncoms. I slept like a baby. A few minutes ago I got up and saw that they had taken their musketoons and gear. I went to the stables and twelve horses are gone. They tuk enough for mounts and three besides for carrying water and food."

"Do ye think we can run them down?"

Hallahan's face tightened. "Out there, Dan? Klij-Litzogue owns that country, and well ye know it. Besides, there is something else ye should know."

"Go on."

"Ye'd best come to the stables."

Hallahan lighted a lantern he took from a hook near the door and led the way along the low-roofed stables. He stopped at a stall. "Take a look at Big Pat," he said quietly.

Gallagher walked into the stall, spoke softly to the big bay, and then took the lantern from Hallahan. He held it up to study the horse. There was a pussy discharge from the nose and eyes, and the eyes were inflamed. "Jesus God," said Gallagher. He looked at Hallahan. "Is it mayhap farcy, do ye think?"

Hallahan slowly shook his head. " 'Tis glanders, Dan."

"And the rest of the mounts?"

"*All* of them, Dan. They have fever and swollen lymph glands, and they all have lost weight. There is only one exception. The captain's bay, Shannon. Ye know we keep him in a special stall in the old storehouse beside the corral because he fights with the other stallions."

Gallagher walked out of the stall and to the outer door without looking back at the dying animals. They would *all* die. If it had been farcy, a milder form of glanders, they would live, although still infected, but this was not so, according to Mike Hallahan, and no man knew horses better then he did.

Gallagher placed the lantern on the ground.

Hallahan. "We'll have to burn the stables, Dan."

Gallagher did not answer. Hallahan did not know of the dispatch that would send all of them to their deaths in the distant Diablos, on *foot* now.

Hallahan looked to the east where the growing light of day was etching the wolf-fanged mountains darkly against the coming of the sun. "What do we do now, Dan?"

Gallagher quietly told him of the orders.

Hallahan wiped the sweat from his face. "To go there is to die, Dan."

"Aye."

"But there is nothing else we can do."

"No."

"It has been a long trail together, Dan."

Gallagher nodded. "Where is Sergeant Caris?"

"In the hospital, Dan. Taken hard with fever he was."

Gallagher looked quickly at Hallahan. "When was this?"

"Yesterday. He is not the only one."

"How many others?"

Hallahan hesitated. "Corporal Nellis is down too, and Privates Carmody, Dudzik, Jonas, Barents and Schiel."

"Typhoid?"

"I think so."

Gallagher felt the invisible belly blows of fate. He wiped his face with his bandana. "And Mister Tyrel?"

"Bad, Dan, very bad."

"Is there nothing good?"

"Only a man's duty, Dan."

There were no officers left, fit to do their duty. There were no horses to carry the company on its mission. There was hardly anything left of the company.

"What are your orders, Sergeant?" asked Hallahan.

Gallagher straightened up. He was the first soldier. The man with the three stripes and the diamond. The ramrod placed against the spine of the company. Gallagher was not afflicted with typhoid, gangrene, or alcoholism. He wasn't licked yet. He grinned wryly. Poor consolation that was.

"Sergeant?"

Gallagher turned. "Have the trumpeter blow first call."

"There is hardly a squad left to answer it, Sergeant."

"Blow it!"

Gallagher strode toward headquarters, and as he entered he heard Hallahan's voice blasting Trumpeter Farrington out of his bunk.

The sun was well up. The shooting was over. The corpses of the diseased horses lay at the bottom of the deep cleft just south of the post boundaries. It had been more merciful to kill them while they were still on their legs. But nothing is more painful to a horse soldier than to have to kill his mount.

The typhoid had almost full control now. The rations had been poor for some time, with very little variety. The men had been weakened by their substandard diet, and the disease had caught hold. None of the sick could be moved. There were no horses to move them. There were not enough men left on their feet to guard them if they *were* on the move. If they stayed at the fort, and there was nothing else they could do, the few men able to fight would hardly be enough to hold off an Apache attack.

Gallagher had had charges placed in the various buildings—enough to destroy them and not harm the hospital. A detail had been piling extra equipment together in the big corral down the slope from the stables. It was equipment that could not be moved. Yet all of Gallagher's preparations seemed useless to him. The whole bloody business seemed useless. What more could be expected of him?

He walked to the edge of the post and looked to the west, toward the invisible Diablos. Heat waves shimmered and danced across the flats. After the cold night it had suddenly become unseasonably warm, almost like summer, but that would not last. He walked the boundaries of the post buildings, slowly, lost in thought, trying to find some way of obeying his commander's last orders, but he could not.

He stopped on the low rise to the east of the post and looked across the low country below the mesa. There was a faint suggestion of dust far out there. Perhaps a wind devil. It would not be Apaches. They would not herald their approach with banners of yellow dust.

He walked back in headquarters. It was quiet in there. The company guidon rested in its stand against the wall behind the company commander's desk. Gallagher studied it. He had ridden behind it for ten years and had heard it snap in the dry winds of summer and the icy blasts of winter. He had seen its bright colors against the dun of the sterile desert and against the lush green of the mountains.

The guidon was swallow-tailed, colored half red and half white, and attached to a nine-foot lance. The white letters "U. S." were emblazoned on the red upper half, and the red letter "A" was on the white lower half. The captain's last order had been that the guidon should be returned to the regiment where it belonged, *after* the mission had been accomplished.

"How?" asked Gallagher quietly. He threw up his hands in a gesture of despair.

Mister Tyrel shot himself at sundown—twenty-two years old, with but six months service on the frontier. He was a soldier, but not yet a true dragoon. He would be buried next to Captain D'Arcy Eustis who had served his country well for over thirty years and had died forgotten, still wearing the blue. The long trail from the United States Military Academy, the Seminole War, the Mexican War, as well as years of duty in Indian-fighting country had ended for him at forgotten Fort McComber.

The darkness that night was complete. Beyond the faint yellow lights in the hospital and guardhouse there was nothing but blackness . . . and the howling of the wind. Three men died of typhoid in the hours before dawn.

Gallagher awoke to see gray light creeping in through the windows of the headquarters office. He got up from his cot and pulled on his shell jacket and shoes. Another day of indecision. What was the use of trying to keep this parody of a military post going?

It was much lighter when boots thudded against the wooden porch in front of the headquarters and the door swung open. Gallagher turned from the window where he had been looking to the east, to where he had seen that threadlike and persistent line of yellow dust the day before until dusk had hidden it.

Lieutenant Artenis stood there. His face was pale beneath the tan, but the man was sober.

"Good morning, sir," said Gallagher.

Artenis nodded. "The dispatches?"

"On the captain's desk, sir."

"How is he, Sergeant?"

Gallagher stared at the officer for a moment. "He is dead, sir."

The brown eyes flicked up. "Is Mister Tyrel any better?"

"Mister Tyrel is dead, too, sir. Gangrene." There was no sense in saying "suicide", and clouding the memory of a dead man. Gallagher had entered it on the books as death by gangrene, brought on by the poisoned arrow of an Apache. Maybe it really didn't make any difference. Maybe no one would ever know either way, for it seemed as though every man and everything at Fort McComber would be lost with no record.

Artenis sat down and looked through the dispatches. He spent a long time reading the vital one, then walked to the map on the wall and studied it. Gallagher watched him. There was something odd about the man. At last Artenis turned. "There is no question of this dispatch being obeyed of course, Sergeant."

"The lieutenant is now in command. Captain Eustis' last command was that the order was to be carried out."

"Corporal Hallahan told me about the horses."

Gallagher nodded.

"Then you agree that it is hopeless to carry out this order?"

"It is the *lieutenant's* decision, sir."

"Then it will *not* be carried out."

"Yes, sir."

"What's wrong with you, Gallagher?"

"Nothing . . . , sir."

Artenis looked through the window. "There is no hope

THE BORDER GUIDON

for any Union troops in Arizona now that the Confederates have invaded New Mexico and Arizona. It is my intention to surrender this post to them."

Gallagher glanced at the guidon.

Artenis did not turn. "We are not far from the route the Confederates will take to the west. There is no hope for us at this time with typhoid raging here, no horses, and not enough men to defend the post."

Gallagher wet his lips and waited.

"I want you to bear witness that the situation here was impossible, in case there is a military court, Sergeant."

Gallagher eyed the straight back of the officer. There was something else coming. Gallagher could feel it.

Artenis turned slowly. "I intend to surrender the fort. At that time I will resign my commission in the United States Army and take service under the Confederate States of America."

That was it! That was what had been bothering the man all this time. It had not been the typhoid at all.

"Well, Sergeant?"

Gallagher eyed the man. "Why do ye wait until then to resign?"

The brown eyes half closed. "What difference does it make?"

"If ye turn over this post as an officer of the United States Army, then resign and take service with the Confederacy, ye will stand trial for treason if ye are captured by the United States forces."

"If," said Artenis quietly.

"Suit yerself, lieutenant."

Artenis rubbed his freshly shaven cheeks. He eyed Gallagher. There was a glint of fear in his eyes. There was a sneaky streak in the man. Suddenly he sat down and began to write. He signed the sheet with a flourish and sanded it. He looked up at Gallagher. "This is my resignation."

"Ye want me to witness it?"

"Not yet."

"Why, sir?"

Artenis smiled. "Look out of that window."

It was light enough for Gallagher to see that mysterious wraith of dust once more.

"Those are Texas mounted rifles, Gallagher. On their way here to occupy this post."

"So?"

"I have known for some time they were coming here."

"So."

Artenis leaned back in his chair. "I have already been offered a commission in that command."

"The lieutenant was pretty quiet about that fact when the captain was still alive."

"There was a reason."

"I can imagine." Gallagher closed his hands into great hard fists. "We have been at war with the Confederacy for ten months. Why did ye not resign at the beginning av the war?"

Artenis toyed with the letter opener on the desk. "Did you know what duty I was assigned to just before I joined this company?"

"No, sir."

The brown eyes had a glint in them. "Until I came here to Fort McComber, I was quartermaster officer at Fort Coulter."

The impact of Artenis' statement hit Gallagher like an Apache lance—the transshipment of arms and munitions from Fort Coulter to Fort Breckenridge to Fort Craig, where the boxes were opened and found to be filled with rocks and sand.

"Do you get the idea, Gallagher?"

"I do."

Artenis smiled. "Clever, was it not?"

"Aye."

The officer leaned forward. "There is one thing I want to point out to you. You are an experienced soldier. The Confederacy needs men like you who know this country. There could be a commission in it for you. The Confederacy is not as fussy as the United States. They do not require a man to be an officer *and* a gentleman."

"Like *ye*, belike?"

Artenis flushed. "I can get you a commission. We can

use you, Gallagher. We must pass through the country of Klij-Litzogue to get those weapons and munitions. You can guide us. You are the only man who can guide us. What do you say?"

"Ye have no else to do it? Ye cannot do it yourself?"

"No," admitted the officer.

Gallagher breathed out and stepped closer to the desk. " 'Tis a deal," he said firmly. He leaned forward. "Let me see that resignation."

Artenis handed it to him. Gallagher read it. It was right and proper. He took a pen, and before Artenis could stop him he had signed it as witness. He folded it, placed it inside his jacket, then smiled coldly at Millard Artenis. "Get up," he said.

"What do you mean?"

"Get up, ye traitorous bastard!"

"You're talking to an officer!"

Gallagher smiled again, tapped his jacket, and reached for the officer with great eager hands. "Ye *were* an officer, Artenis."

He dragged him clear across the desk, set him up, hit him in the belly and then on the jaw, and drove him crashing into a corner. He butted him with his head when he came up, hooked vicious blows to belly and jaw, then stood over the bleeding writhing man waiting for him to get up.

The door banged open and Mike Hallahan came in. He stared at Gallagher. "Ye've gone loco with the strain, Dan!"

Gallagher shook his head. He reached down for Artenis and raised him easily to his feet. Tenderly he braced him, smiled benignly into the battered and bleeding face, then hit him with a terrific one-two that drove the officer clear across the room and over a chair. Gallagher turned and dusted his hands.

Hallahan stared at Gallagher and then backed slowly toward the door. "Wait," said Gallagher. He took out the resignation and handed it to Hallahan, then swiftly explained what had happened.

Hallahan looked at the dust on the desert to the east. "What happens now?" he said. "We'll have to surrender."

Gallagher shook his head. "Not all of us, Mike."

"What do you mean?"

Gallagher looked at Artenis. "I'm senior noncom here. There are no officers. I'm leaving to ride to Fort Coulter on the captain's fine bay Shannon, and I'm going to find and destroy them stores."

"I knew yer mind was gone."

"Ye will stay here in command. Fire the extra stores lying in the corral. Destroy anything they can use. Keep food and medical supplies for yer men. With the honors av war, the ribils will not harm ye. I'm sorry it has to be this way, Mike."

Hallahan nodded. "Aye, Dan." He gripped Gallagher by the hand. "If any man can do it ye can." But the lie was in his eyes. He knew and Dan knew that the odds were insurmountable and that Dan Gallagher was only making a defiant gesture in the face of a grinning fate.

They worked swiftly after that. Hallahan got Shannon and saddled him. He packed rations and water and Mister Tyrel's fine Sharps carbine, as well as a brace of extra Colts. He had it all ready in twenty minutes.

Gallagher went to the captain's quarters and looked about. There was little he could take. But he must have something. Not the violin, of course. The dueling pistols were enticing but hardly worth the weight of them on such a mission. He saw a small velvet case on the mantel and took it and opened it. The lovely faces of three young girls looked up at him. He whistled softly. One of them, evidently the oldest, looked enough like the old man to be his daughter, and then the resemblance of her and the next oldest of the three girls struck him. They must be the daughters of D'Arcy Eustis. He closed the case and slipped it inside his jacket. He left the room hurriedly and returned to headquarters. Artenis was still unconscious. Gallagher grinned. He took the dispatch box and walked to the door. Suddenly he turned and looked at the guidon. That had been part of the orders, too. He took it from its stand and left the office.

Hallahan watched Gallagher attach the guidon by butt socket and leathern sling to his saddle. Gallagher mounted and looked down at Hallahan. They did not speak but gripped hands. Then Gallagher kneed the big bay away from the corporal and rode to the west. He did not see the smart salute given to his broad back by Corporal Michael Hallahan, nor did he see the growing pillar of dust rising from the east side of the mesa.

A little while later a thread of smoke arose from Fort McComber as Hallahan fired the stores. It grew and grew until it was like a huge funereal pall against the clear sky, and the Tontos who saw it wondered at it, but they did not approach the post. There were white-eyes riding toward the fort—men in gray uniforms instead of blue ones, and whose speech was different from that of the men in blue. The blues and the grays had many things in common: the set jaw, the hard look, and the easy familiarity with firearms that no Apache could ever hope to attain.

▶▶ *Chapter* 5

THE DYING sun seemed snagged on the rimrock, and the hollows in the desert and on the mountainside had filled with lilac-hued shadows. The dull leaden shapes of the mountains seemed to brood over the desolation below them. In all that vast area there was no sign of life but for the lone man who led the big bay horse to the west. The dry wind that swept over the malpais fluttered the swallow-tailed guidon at the end of its lance.

By rights there should have been thirty-five or forty dragoons riding behind that guidon, but the big redheaded man who led the bay was utterly alone in a country where such loneliness had often driven white men mad.

Dan Gallagher raised his tired head. He had been walking for hours to let the bay rest and yet it seemed as though the western hills were no closer than they had been when he had entered the malpais country early that morning, with Fort McComber two days behind him.

He looked back at the bay. "Shannon," he said quietly, "I'm after thinking we're on a treadmill."

The dark bay tossed his proud head. Gallagher unhooked one of the three canteens from his saddle and shook it. There was hardly enough water to make a sloshing noise. It was the last of the gamey stuff he had patiently strained through his neck scarf the evening before from a rock pan where a diamondback rattler had decided to end it all.

He poured the water into his battered Fra Diabolo hat and let the bay drink while he himself touched his cracked lips with his tongue and looked west across the harsh naked country. There was really nothing to look at, nothing more than he had seen all day long. The heat from the baking rock beneath his feet came up through the soles of his shoes. That morning he had thought he knew where he was. Now he wasn't so sure. Certainly he was heading west, but he had no sure idea of how far south he was.

The bay finished drinking and looked at Gallagher almost as though to say, "I've had enough. Now it's your turn, Gallagher."

He filled his mouth with the gamey water that was left, swilled it about his mouth, then let it flow back into the canteen. "How far south?" he said aloud. "Apaches to the west and south. Ribils to the east. Unknown country to the north. A redheaded Irishman betwixt and between them, and all of them, including this cursed country, looking for his heart's blood!"

He placed the wet hat on his head, grateful for the temporary coolness of it, hooked the canteen to the saddle, then led the bay on again. The gaunt shadows of man and horse moved slowly along the harsh ground, with the fluttering shadow of the guidon above them.

The sun was almost gone when he saw the smoke. He halted and slitted his burning eyes. It was hardly visible, a faint line of darkness against the sky. Apaches in all likelihood. No white man in his right mind would betray himself in that country by lighting a fire. Gallagher took the Sharps carbine from its saddle sling and checked load and cap.

The wind shifted, bringing a new coldness with it, sweeping dust and harsh grit like a great rough broom, raking both man and horse without pity. The sun died even as they stood there. The thick darkness before the rising of the new moon would soon fill the country. Ahead of him were the first of the low, gaunt hills, like loose elephant skin lying atop the basic rock of the land. There was a pass through those hills, or at least he had seen a notch which might, or might not be a pass. It didn't make much difference. He *had* to go that way.

It was black night when he entered the first defile of the pass, and the coldness seemed to close in on him like icy clutching hands. The shoes of the bay struck against the rock and seemed to echo like cathedral bells.

The bushy-haired devils didn't fight at night. That thought at least was good. But they'd track him all night if they had caught sight of him during his march to the hills across the open malpais country, then gut him with a knife at first dawn light. Or maybe, if they had the time and the inclination, they'd haul him home to the squaws for a little clean and happy sport. He was a big powerful man who'd likely live a long time under the razor-edged knives and the burning brands. There were other things they'd do, too, and the chill thought of them sickened him.

The moon was tinting the eastern sky with silvery light when at last Gallagher reached the western end of the winding pass. He was higher now than when he had entered it. A low plain stretched to the west, where a mass of mountains etched against the sky. He reached back and got his carbine, then loosened the holster flaps on the pair of pistols that hung heavy from his lean waist. Thirteen rounds between him and the enemy—twelve for the enemy and one for himself, if it came to that.

The bay whinnied softly. Gallagher raised his head quickly. "Is it water ye smell, Shannon?"

There was a darker patch of something in the darkness ahead. "Trees, by God!" said Gallagher.

Where there were trees there would be water, but where there was water there might also be Apaches. They knew the white man's ways. He'd head for water like a thirsty sheep and stay near it while he camped, and like a sheep he could thus be slain easily.

The wind shifted, and Gallagher caught a strong smell of smoke. There was a red pinpoint of motion among the trees like a winking eye. The wind had fanned embers into life again. The fire flared up, casting an eerie flickering light on what looked to the Gallagher like a long stretch of fire-blackened wall. He rubbed his bristly jaws. This part of the country was unknown to him. He knew it well enough to the north and also further south, but this was no man's land as far as he knew. He had never heard of white people living in the area.

Thirst and hunger had allied themselves in a winning

THE BORDER GUIDON 43

battle against man and horse. It was almost a certainty that there wasn't any water within marching distance of the next day or so, and hardly any game to speak of. A big man and a big horse needed lots of food. Red meat for the man, grain for the horse. Most of all, they needed water.

Gallagher moved on, keeping to the low places and always watching—first to right and left, then behind, then ahead, and never stopping. To stop looking was to die . . . quickly.

He was three hundred yards from the trees when he stopped and ground-reined the bay. He padded quietly forward, surprisingly quiet for a man his size. The moon was higher now, and he could make out the structures amongst the trees. A well-built place from the looks of it, but why was it there, with no stage route through that country and no mining to speak of? The place was quiet, too quiet. There was no sound of mule or horse, no bark of dog or sound of human voice.

The wind flared up the fire, and he could see something humped lying on the ground near the wide arched gateway that led into the rectangle of buildings. A mule. A dead mule. Someone had cut deep into the flanks to rip out steaks. Gallagher felt his red hair stiffen a little, and he almost reached up to settle his hat. Appaches liked horse meat, but they liked sweet mule meat much better. If they stole horses and mules they usually killed the mules for meat.

Gallagher squatted behind a rock like a big joss idol. He was damned if he went in there and damned if he didn't. He had to have water and food. If he by-passed this place he might go on until he and the bay dropped, easy prey for the Apaches, the buzzards, or both. He peered around the rock. The moonlight touched something else. Just beyond the mule, next to some brush, lay a dead man. One clawed hand was outstretched as though he was reaching for the mutilated mule. The man's head was curiously misshapen. Some kindly warrior had let out the man's spirit by crushing his skull. Dan stood up. It was a good sign, for Dan in any case. No Apaches would stay around the newly dead at night and wait for the wandering soul to speak with the weird voice of Bú, the owl.

He padded forward, with his carbine held at chest height, while his hard blue eyes probed the shadows. But there was nothing, no sound or movement beyond the muted crackling of the fire. He saw a great blackened spot where one of the larger buildings had burned to the ground. There were embers of fire upon it like rubies on black velvet. Here and there were twisted lengths of blackened metal.

He stopped in the shelter of a big niche cut into the high wall that surrounded most of the buildings. The pair of massive and bolt-studded gates lay flat upon the hard caliche of the compound within the wall. He eyed the windows and doors of the buildings one by one. Nothing. . . .

Debris, dust, and ashes lay in the thin windrows against the walls. A pall of smoke hung over the area. Another dead man lay close to a building, both his hands tangled in the front of his bloody shirt, grasping an arrow shaft embedded in his chest.

Gallagher moved softly, keeping close to the buildings where the shadows still clung, until he reached the far end of the rectangle of buildings. An open-fronted blacksmith's shop was there. It was fully equipped. Gallagher nodded. The Apaches had touched nothing in the shop. Now he was *sure* it was Apaches who had raided the place.

The water was across the compound. It bubbled up from a rock-walled pool. His throat felt as though it had been sanded, and he couldn't resist walking toward the pool. He stopped short when he saw her, at the bottom of the pool, naked as the day she had been born. Her long dark hair floated about her ivory shoulders with the slow movement of the water. Her great staring eyes seemed to look directly at Gallagher as though to mesmerize him. The ugly wound that had caused her death showed at the left side of her shapely throat. There was a faint pinkish hue to the water about it. She had not been dead long.

Gallagher did not want to look ar her. She had been lovely, and the strange, eerie feeling that he had seen her somewhere before entered his mind.

He stepped back, one slow step after another, until his back struck a building. He turned and walked to a door, which swung easily open on its hinges at his touch. He peered into the thick darkness within. His thirst was worse now that he had seen the clear fresh water of the spring; water that he could not drink . . . for a time, at least. Later, he'd take her out of there and give her a Christian burial. But until he found the next waterhole or spring, wherever and whenever that would be, he would have a hell of a time stomaching the water he would take from this place of the dead.

He stepped softly into the room and peered about like a wary animal. He could almost feel his ears slant forward. His eyes gradually grew accustomed to the moonlit darkness. The place was a shambles. The floor was littered with ripped clothing, some of it blood stained, shattered furniture, smashed glass and crockery.

He touched his cracked lips with his tongue. There was a cabinet in a corner, and he opened it. The faint odor of spirits came to him, but the cabinet was empty. As he stepped back his left spur rang softly against glass or crockery. Likely a damned chamberpot, he thought sourly. He looked down and saw the square bottle. He picked it up and pulled out the cork with his teeth. The fruity odor struck him sweetly. "By all the saints," he said with a smile. " 'Tis brandy!"

It went down easily, then hit his empty stomach and tired brain at the same time. He sat down quickly on a chair. The second slug settled him a bit, and the third did the trick. He was just loosening his shell jacket when the cold thought came to him that his horse was still out there. Apaches might be watching the place. They wouldn't enter it that night. Still, he hadn't found any food, and if he did have to leave in a hurry he'd need it.

He sloshed the brandy about in the bottle, then raised it

toward his lips. It was then that he heard, or seemingly felt, the faint noise from the next room, beyond a closed door.

Gallagher slowly got to his feet. His breath seemed abnormally loud to him. He softly placed the bottle on a table and eyed the door. He stood there a long time before he heard a slight coughing noise. Belike a baby, he thought. His face muscles tightened. *Apaches coughed, too.*

The door latch moved a trifle, and then the door swung open with a slight sighing of hinges. Someone stood there staring at Gallagher, but not for long. One hundred and ninety pounds of tough bone and muscle struck with pile-driver power, driving back and back until both Gallagher and his quarry struck against a light table and sent it smashing against the far wall. A knife traced a burning course down Gallagher's left bicep, and he dropped his carbine to hook a shoulder into the belly of his opponent. The belly was not cord-tough like that of a warrior, but soft and full.

Gallagher fell on top of the fiercely fighting, still unseen enemy. The knife scraped across his pistol belt. He felt for the wrist, twisted it sharply, and heard the knife tinkle against the packed earth floor. A knee drove up into his groin, and he gasped in swift agony, rolling free to get to his knees. His left hand felt cloth and he gripped at it. Something ripped cleanly, and he felt the weight of a garment in his hand. A dim white figure scrambled to its feet. The mingled odor of scent and femininity came to Gallagher. His mouth gaped open. "By the powers!" he gasped. "A woman!"

She slowly moved back toward the wall.

"I'm white, ma'am," said Gallagher foolishly. "A soldier." The burning thought of that soft body stayed with him. He had not been with a woman for a long time.

The blood ran down his arm and dripped from his fingers. He placed a hand on the table, found a candle lying there, quickly drew out a block of matches and thumbed one of them into life.

"Don't light that candle!" she cried out.

THE BORDER GUIDON 47

It was too late. The candle flared up and he looked at her across the yellow flickering light. The dancing play of light was on her naked body, throwing the high breasts into full relief. Her dark hair flowed over her smooth shoulders. The reddened knife was again in her hand, and she held it toward Gallagher.

Gallagher looked down at the clothing he had ripped from her. It was a gingham dress. "I. . . ." His voice trailed off. He pinched out the light of the candle and tossed the dress to her as he hurriedly walked from the room.

The bottle was waiting for him. He took a stiff jolt. His arm burned like fury. He rolled up the sleeve and saw a long shallow gash in the hard flesh. He peeled off his shell jacket and undershirt.

The door swung open behind him. "I'll take care of that," she said quietly. "After all, *I* did it."

"I'd be obliged, ma'am."

She came to him in the moonlight, the dress covering the nakedness he had seen but not the sweet curves of her body. She lighted a candle and took the bottle from his hand. She poured some of the brandy into the wound.

"What a waste!" he protested.

She looked up at him with her dark violet eyes. "You're Irish," she said.

He grinned. "And what else could I be now, ma'am?"

She took a clean cloth from a rack and tore it into long strips which she used to neatly bandage his arm. "You'll live," she said quietly.

She looked up at him, deep-seated fear etched on her pale face. Then she placed her head against his chest, and the dry sobs broke from her like a torrent.

He was sure he had seen this girl, too, somewhere in the past. In Boston or New York? St. Louis or Santa Fe? He half closed his eyes. There was one thing he did know. She looked uncommonly like the girl who lay cold in death at the bottom of the pool. "Ah God," he said softly.

Chapter 6

"You can relight the candles," he said over his shoulder as he finished hanging cloth over the last of the windows. He stepped down from the chair and looked at her as the light filled the room. Try as he would he could not forget her white flesh and the cups of her breasts as he had seen them.

She took her soft lower lip between even white teeth and glanced nervously at the door.

"They will not come," he said quietly.

"Why not?"

"Because of the dead. The vengeance of the spirits. They are even afraid of their own dead until they are laid to by the *diyis,* the medicine men and medicine women. That is why they will not stay near owls. They think Bú, the owl, speaks with the voice of the newly dead."

She sat down and began to mend her dress with pins and ties of cloth. "You seem to know a great deal about them, Sergeant."

"Some," he admitted. "There is one thing I do not know about them."

"And that is?"

He picked up a chair, twirled it, and then sat down in it. "What happened here. I am First Sergeant Daniel Gallagher, Provisional Company A, First United States Dragoons. Ye can call me Dan."

She looked up quickly from her mending. "Company A? But they are in New Mexico or perhaps traveling east to the war." She leaned forward. "They were at Fort McComber some months ago, were they not?"

He studied her. "How is it ye know so much about the company?"

"Because it is commanded by my father, Captain D'Arcy Eustis. I am Ellen Eustis."

Gallagher's lower jaw dropped. Pieces of a once-vague puzzle began to drop into place. Instinctively his right hand touched the place inside his jacket where he had placed the small velvet-covered picture case he had taken from the captain's quarters just before leaving Fort McComber.

"I came here with my two sisters Evelyn and Judith from California. We were told we could get no further east, that all United States troops had left Arizona, that there were Apaches on the warpath from the Colorado to the Rio Grande."

"They are," he said quietly. The girl in the pool was her sister all right. *But where was the third sister?*

"If you are first sergeant of my father's company you must know where he is and how he is."

Gallagher found it difficult to meet her gaze. "Yes," he said in a low voice.

"Then tell me!"

He stood up. "Of course. But we will need water for coffee."

"What coffee?"

He smiled. "The coffee I will make." He picked up a kettle for the water and reached for his carbine.

"Wait," she said as she arose.

Gallagher turned. "Well?"

"Are any of them out there?"

"Apaches?"

Her face was deathly pale. "I mean . . . white people."

The candle guttered in the draft as he opened the door a little.

"Answer me," she said.

He turned his head. "There are white people out there," he said slowly and distinctly, "but they are not for ye to see, ma'am."

A hand crept up to the smooth column of her throat. "Are any of them women?"

He opened the door a little more.

"Well, Sergeant?"

"Yes," he said at last. "There is a woman out there."

"There are three of us," she said, "as I told you. Evelyn, Judith, and myself. Evelyn is a little younger than I am and looks like my twin. Judith is smaller and blonde."

It was Evelyn in the pool then. "Ye must not follow me," he said quietly.

"One woman. Which is it, Sergeant?"

"The one that looks like ye."

"Evelyn, then." There was a long pause. "Take me to her."

"No."

"I insist!"

He turned slowly. "Ye can insist all ye like, but ye will stay here until I return."

"Is she dead?"

"Yes. But she must have died quickly. It does not look like she was abused." He walked outside and closed the door behind him. He heard a soft muted crying from inside the room.

He walked to the pool and looked at her. He hated to have to touch the body, but he could not leave her there. He could not allow Ellen to see her. He reached into the cold water and touched her. He looked away as he pulled her body from the pool and cradled it in his arms. He carried it into one of the buildings and placed it on a cot, then covered it with a rough blanket. His breath came harshly in this throat, and he felt the green bile rise. He left the room and wedged the door shut with a billet of wood.

Gallagher walked to the gateway with his carbine ready in his big hands. He looked across the moonlit plain. Nothing moved. Shadows of brush and rock were etched like black ink on the silvery earth. "There were three of us," she had said. "Evelyn, Judith, and myself."

He knew where Ellen was, and Evelyn, but where was Judith? God alone knew that.

Gallagher walked out onto the plain, damned conscious of his size and long shadow on the naked ground. Each step was like a step up the gallows ladder until he heard

THE BORDER GUIDON

Shannon softly winny. He walked to the stallion and rested his head against its neck. He led the bay toward the buildings, and each ring of hoof on that hard earth sounded like a chapel bell when the Black Mass was to be celebrated.

His heart was thudding as he led the bay into the compound and let him trot eagerly toward the pool. He could not bear to watch him drink there.

He found a butt of fresh water in one of the smaller buildings. There was a body in the room, too, that of a young boy. They had had a little sport with him before they had killed him. He had been just a little too old for them to take him for adoption. There was pure hell in Gallagher's eyes as he turned away from the body.

She was straightening up the room when he entered it. She did not speak, but as she looked at him there was a question in her eyes.

"I did not see Judith," he said at last. "I'll look about a bit while ye make the coffee."

"There is none to be found," she said. Her eyes never left his.

"A good dragoon is never without his coffee," he said. He took a small bag of the beans from his pocket.

"That is not the way the song goes," she said absentmindedly.

He squinted at her in the yellow light. "So? Ye know the song, then?"

"Yes. It says a good dragoon is never without his horse, his liquor, and his woman."

Gallagher grinned. He reached for his carbine. "Start the fire. But use only dry wood."

"They'll see the smoke, Sergeant."

"Aye, but it doesn't really matter."

"What do you mean?"

He looked quickly at her, his eyes as hard as glacier ice. "If they are close enough to see the smoke they are close enough to have seen me come here. If they are *not* that close then it doesn't matter, does it?"

"You're a fatalist, then?"

He drew out one of his pistols and began to pound

the coffee beans with the butt of it. "I have been on the frontier a long time following the guidon av the First Dragoons. There were only a handful of us out here on the frontier, perhaps one soldier against a thousand savages, if ye want to quote the odds. A man gets a little fatalistic with such odds."

"You don't have to stay in the Army, Sergeant."

He shrugged, "It is my way av life. There was nothing left in Ireland except starvation. Ireland's best export seems to be her men. They have fought all over the world under many flags. Every flag, it seems, except their own."

"Are you a mercenary?"

He finished with the beans and handed her the bag. "A fighting man, yes; a mercenary, no. I am American the same as ye, miss."

She flushed. "You were going to tell me of my father."

He stood up and shoved back his hat. "Aye."

She eyed him expectantly.

"When was the last time ye heard from him?" he asked.

"Some time last summer. At that time he expected to be transferred to California."

He nodded. "Aye. We started out, but the orders were changed."

"Then we heard he was in New Mexico, at Santa Fe."

"We were there for a time."

"He wanted us to join him. We thought we would surprise him. We took ship for San Francisco early last fall. The ship was damaged rounding Cape Horn, and we put into Callao for repairs. Then a fever epidemic started, and we did not reach San Francisco until December. I wrote to him from there before we started south. At Los Angeles we managed to join a party of traders and merchants bound for New Mexico. They did not know the Apaches held control of this territory. They decided to go to Sonora and then find their way north into New Mexico. They would not take us, saying it was too dangerous."

"They were right."

She poked up the crackling fire. "We hired guides to this place, and here we stayed. We could not go ahead, nor could we return, and we had no idea of where my father was. There was a rumor that his company had gone to Santa Fe and then to the East. We did not know."

Gallagher remembered the letter he had found in the dispatch case, addressed in feminine handwriting to the captain, in care of Fort Marcy, Santa Fe, New Mexico Territory.

"Where is he now, Sergeant?"

Gallagher felt the cold sweat break out on his forehead. Before God, she had taken enough of a beating with the death of one sister and the loss of the other. How could he tell her?

"Sergeant Gallagher?"

Gallagher touched his cracked lips with his tongue. She was alone, in the heart of hostile country, with nothing to look forward to but death, or a worse fate amongst the Apaches.

"Sergeant Gallagher!"

Wordlessly he took the velvet-covered picture case and the stained envelope from his jacket and handed them to her. She looked down at them. "This picture case. We sent it to him some years ago. How is it you have it . . . and the letter?"

"I left your father but two days ago," he said. He held up a hand at the look in her fine eyes. "There is no use in lying to ye. Ye are a soldier's daughter. Yer father passed away of typhoid fever, miss. He was on duty to the last. A fine man and soldier."

She slowly placed the letter and the case on the table and looked away from Gallagher. For a few moments she stood there, and then she spoke over her shoulder. "What will they do with her?"

She was her father's daughter, all right. She had suffered two terrible losses, but she was still alive and was now the head of the family, small as it was. Her concern now was for the living, not the dead of blessed memory.

"Judith? I do not know."

"Don't lie to me."

He leaned against the wall and felt for his pipe and tobacco. He filled the pipe and lighted it. "They are impulsive," he said at last. "There are times when they kill everything in sight like a spoiled child smashing his toys. There are other times when they take captives. Not grown men, ye understand, for they are always dangerous, and the Apache takes no chances. Small children are usually adopted or held for ransom. Some of those that are adopted, Americans or Mexicans, grow up as Apaches, and they sometimes get worse than their foster people. Men and older boys are usually killed." He puffed at his pipe and blew out the fragrant smoke. He watched the smoke ring waver and then drift toward a window. "How old is she?"

"Eighteen."

He said nothing. Most Apache women were married long before reaching that age. To them an eighteen-year-old was a fully grown woman, and if they did not take her with them to become a squaw they would have their way with her. *All* of them; half a dozen bucks or half a hundred. What would be left, if it was alive, would hardly want to live.

"There isn't much hope then, is there?" she asked.

"Quien sabe?"

"You don't like to give up, do you?"

He shrugged.

"It happened so quickly. Mister Dunlap was kind to us. This is . . . was . . . his place. He told us there was nothing to fear when we saw the smoke signals in the hills. The Apaches had never bothered him before. During times of peace he had treated some of their sick and injured. He thought that would save all of us."

"He was a good man, but either a fool or exceptionally brave," said Gallagher dryly. "It is all right to treat their sick and injured, *providing* they recover, but if they do not . . ."

She passed a hand across her forehead, brushing back her dark hair. "Mister Dunlap was trying to figure out some way to help us. Everything was so vague, so uncertain. He sent a messenger to Fort McComber several days after we got here with a message to my father."

Gallagher shook his head. "No messenger ever came from here to Fort McComber," he said.

"He said he would take us to Fort Coulter if he could not get word through to my father."

Gallagher eyed her quickly. "Fort Coulter?" He shook his head.

"What do you mean?"

"Fort Coulter has been abandoned since late last fall. Fort McComber is the only occupied post in Arizona." He corrected himself. "At least, it was. If I'm right in what I think, the Stars and Bars now flies over Fort McComber."

"But why would Mister Dunlap agree to take us to Fort Coulter if he knew that it had been abandoned?"

"Aye," said Gallagher dryly. *"Why would he?"*

She paced back and forth. "There were times when I *was* a little suspicious of him. He looked at Judith at times with more than just appreciation for her beauty."

"So?"

"He was drinking one evening and pretended that he was just being fatherly with her." The great violet eyes looked at Gallagher. "I did not think so. But there was little I could do. We were at his mercy, so to speak. There was no other place for us to go."

"Where is he now?"

She stared at him. "Isn't his body out there with the others?"

"I do not know what he looks like, miss."

"A good-sized man, not as wide as you, but perhaps a little taller. Heavily bearded. A large nose and gray eyes. His eyes, well, they seemed as though they could look right through you."

Gallagher rubbed his jaw. "There is no man out there who looks like that."

"It's possible that he might not have been here at the time of the attack."

"Aye."

The coffee had begun to brew, and she waited until it was done, then filled two big granite cups with the liquid.

"How did ye survive the attack?" asked Gallagher as he sipped his coffee.

"I was not with my sisters at the time. I heard Evelyn screaming and ran to get a gun. Then the shooting stopped, and I knew what had happened. I found a knife and ran into this building. In the room where you found me there is an opening through the wall. I suppose they threw firewood into it from the outside, then used it as they needed it from the bin built into the wall. I crawled into it and found myself just outside the walls, hidden by brush which grew alongside the building. I stayed there, listening to them as they finished everyone off...."

He nodded. She had been more than lucky. The picture of her sister's body would remain etched on Gallagher's memory for the rest of his life.

She looked at him. "And you? Where do you come from and where were you going?"

He emptied his cup and refilled it. Then he told her of his mission. She was silent for a long time, and then she looked up at him. "But that is suicide, Sergeant," she said quietly.

"Captain Eustis said *the orders would be obeyed to the letter.* There was one other thing he said ... I have not forgotten it."

"Yes?"

He looked steadily at her. "If there is *one* man left, and *one* only, *that man will return the guidon to the regiment,* Sergeant Gallagher. *But only when the mission has been completed, successfully,* Sergeant Gallagher!"

"And that is what you will do?"

He nodded. "That is what I will do."

"With the territory alive with Apaches? With the Texas mounted rifles to contend with, too? You said they intended to take California."

She was a little startled at the look on his face as he stood up and smashed his right fist into his left palm. "The guidon goes back, under the captain's conditions, if the whole Apache nation and the entire Confederate States of America, as they call themselves, stand in the way!"

"Then you had better leave at once." She walked to the door and opened it, looking back at him. "You still have time to escape. You are a veteran Indian-fighter. You can make it from here alone."

"No," he said flatly.

"I would only burden you."

"That does not matter. You have a right to ask the United States Army for protection."

She could not help but smile. *"One* dragoon?"

He seemed to be twice as big as he really was as he came close to her. *"One* dragoon. That guidon out there goes back to where it belongs. This country belongs to the United States. If there is no other flag for loyal Americans to follow in Arizona they can follow the guidon."

"The Border Guidon," she said softly.

He smiled. "Ye have a way with the words. There must be some Irish in ye! The Border Guidon! I like that!"

"But if the Apaches come back, what then?"

He picked up his carbine. "They will not attack this night. Their favorite time to strike is at the first light of dawn. If they do not come then they will not come at all."

"But would you have gone on alone tonight if you had not found me here?"

"No."

"Don't lie to me, Sergeant!"

"I'm not. The bay is tired. He needs shoeing. There is a blacksmith's shop here. Shannon needs good shoes to carry us back to the blessed Stars and Stripes, wherever that may be."

"You really believe we might make it, don't you?"

He grinned and shook his carbine. "I *know* we can!"

She watched him walk toward the big bay and take the guidon from its socket. He rested it against the wall and then unsaddled the horse. He led it to a stall near the blacksmith's shop.

She walked across to the guidon and lifted the nine-foot lance. The breeze snapped out the little swallow-tailed banner. She eyed it. "I wonder," she whispered into the night.

▶▶ *Chapter* 7

GALLAGHER opened his eyes. The room was still dark, but there was a subtle difference in the night air. It was getting close to dawn. He sat up and glanced toward the girl sleeping quietly on a low couch across the room. He got up and took his carbine. It was cold in the room. He crossed to her with his blanket in his right hand. Her hands rested on her breasts, and her soft lips were slightly parted. Her thick dark hair lay across the pillow. She was a beauty. He covered her with his blanket and left the room.

The compound was still dark, but there was a faint suspicion of dawn light in the eastern sky. A cold wind swept across the area, scattering dried leaves ahead of it. It would not be long before they came. They would come. He was sure of it.

He crossed to the pool, thrust aside his repugnance, and knelt to wash himself in the overflow from the big basin. The water was crystal clear and as cold as ice. Strange that such a spring could exist in so barren a country, but he had seen the same phenomenon in harsher country.

Shannon whinnied from his stall. Gallagher walked softly to the open gateway and looked out across the dark plain. It was quiet except for the swift aimless rushing of the predawn wind. He knew well enough he would never see Apaches until they wanted to be seen. They might very well be within fifty feet of him at that moment, and he'd never know it until they rushed him.

To the west was a wide plain bordered by humped hills. Once in the clear Shannon could outrun any Apache pony. The bay had hunter blood in him. Gallagher was sure he could make it to Fort Yuma on the bay, but with the horse carrying double it would be quite another matter.

Yet they couldn't stay at the station. Not that it wouldn't be pleasant enough, for a time at least. There was food in the storerooms and all the water they'd ever need. A fine looking lass for company, and there might be another bottle or two cached somewhere. A short life and a merry one if they stayed, waiting for the painted death which was sure to come.

He glanced back to the building where she slept, wondering if she'd give in to a man if she knew there was little chance of living more than a few days. "Ah!" said Gallagher, swiping hard at the empty air with his carbine and spitting angrily. "The Devil himself is whisperin' to ye, Gallagher! The lass is a *lady!*"

He walked back to the blacksmith's shop. It was well equipped, and nothing had been disturbed. He started a fire in the forge. It was still too dark for the smoke to be distinguished, and when the charcoal was glowing there would be no smoke at all. But the noise, aye, that would be quite another matter. But the horse could not go on as he was. He could hardly reach the hills before he would be crippled.

It was getting lighter as he walked to the building where she slept. He rapped on the door.

"Come in, Dan," she called out.

She was dressed and freshly washed, her skin glowing and clear. Her thick hair had been drawn together at the nape of her neck and tied with a bright yellow ribbon. Her great eyes searching his face. "Well?" she asked.

"Nothing," he said quietly. "Do not start a fire in here. There is a fire in the forge. Ye can make coffee and do yer cooking there."

"They might see the smoke! They'll certainly hear the noise of the shoeing, Dan!"

He eyed her coldly, and she drew back a little in sudden fear of this big capable man.

"What else is there to do?" he asked at last. He waved a big hand.

She caught the hard anger in his voice and did not answer. She knew his anger was not against her but against the terrible situation they were in.

She took the food to the forge and set to work, trying to forget that they might be surrounded at any moment. He walked into the shop and handed her one of his pistols. "It is loaded and capped," he said. His eyes held hers. "Don't take any chances. If I am cut down or captured do not try to reach me or to fight them off. Even if ye succeeded, which is hardly possible, there would be no way for ye to reach safety.

"Use five of the six rounds if ye must to fight them and to help me, if I need help. But listen to me, lass: *The sixth round is for yerself.* Do ye understand?"

She nodded dumbly and watched him walk toward the gateway trailing his carbine.

He was not in sight as the first light of the false dawn crept above the eastern mountains. The food was almost ready, but he was gone. For a ghastly moment she thought he might have left her and gone on by himself, but then he would not have left the big bay. *Or perhaps they had already caught him.* Her hand grew greasy with cold sweat against the butt of the pistol.

He had not said where her sister was. Evelyn would have to be buried that day. Perhaps she should be washed and laid out, for a little while at least, before she was gone forever.

Ellen walked away from the shop and into a small building. When her eyes grew accustomed to the darkness she saw the body of the boy lying on the floor. Terrified, she left the building and walked across the compound. There, she saw that a door had been wedged shut with a wood billet. She reached for it to take it away.

"Do not go in there," he said from the gateway.

She whirled and raised the pistol in sudden panic.

"Go to the forge," he said in an odd voice.

"But why?"

"Go to the forge!"

The light was clearer as she walked across the compound. She turned to look back at Gallagher, and her blood congealed in her veins. He was not alone.

Fifty yards from him, just outside the gateway, were motionless figures, like demons conjured from the gray light of the morning. She had seen such figures before. The thick manes of hair bound with dingy cloth bands; the broad flat faces with the basilisk eyes. "Dear God," she said. Her legs trembled as she walked. There was no hope for them now. He could not stop them.

They knew Gallagher was the only man there. They knew he was a soldier and would fight with a terrible bloody intensity, and they did not like to lose warriors. They would try to frighten him into surrendering, thought Gallagher. "The bloody bastards," he said between set teeth. He walked into the shop just behind the girl. The forge was a bed of glowing coals. He stripped off shell jacket and undershirt and began to pump the bellows.

She stood with her back pressed against the rear wall. "What will you do? They'll be here any minute!" There was a note of panic in her voice.

He ignored her as he worked. Sweat ran down his broad chest and back as the heat grew. He walked outside with studied deliberation and got the bay. There was no sign of the warriors now, but he knew well enough they were close by.

He began to work steadily, never looking toward the open front of the shop. There could be no escape from them by flight. He heated the horseshoes. His back was toward the shopfront, but he could see her eyes and knew they would warn him when they came.

It took all the iron guts he had to keep on with his work. It wasn't until he turned from the forge to the anvil that he saw how close they were to him, not more than ten feet away, a half dozen of them, with carbines, rifles, and shotguns pointed casually in his direction. One wrong move and he'd be riddled like Aunt Bridget's colander.

They were naked from the waist up despite the coldness of the morning air, wore the buckskin kilt and high desert moccasins tied about their knotty calves. There was no expression on any of the flat faces, and their eyes hardly moved at all.

The girl drew in her breath sharply and then steadied herself at a hard glance from him. There was no need for him to talk. *"Be silent! Don't move! Above all, show no fear,"* his eyes seemed to say.

The short hammer rang steadily against a glowing shoe, and the sparks shot toward the door. The Apaches moved a little. Gallagher seemed intent on his work, and no one could know that the cold sweat of fear ran down his muscular upper body to mingle with the hot sweat of exertion.

The hammer sang a rhythmical song against the glowing metal, the sparks showered steadily, and all the while the big redheaded Irishman seemed so intent on his work that one would have thought he was alone in the shop instead of giving a solo performance for half a dozen of the bloodiest fighters in the entire Southwest.

Another warrior suddenly appeared behind his mates. They stepped aside to let him through, and when Gallagher saw who it was it took all the steel in his belly to keep the strokes of the hammer from faltering. It was Klij-Litzogue. The half-healed wounds on his wide face gave him a look of a demon straight from the honor guard of hell. Gallagher's musketoon had smashed that already fearsome visage into something almost unreal in its terrible hideousness. The flat black eyes looked full into Gallagher's blue ones, and they seemed to clash like striking blades. Then the Tonto's eyes shifted to look at the woman, and he advanced one moccasined foot into the shop.

Gallagher snatched a glowing shoe from the forge and slapped it onto the anvil. There was no time now to do the job right. He had to hammer hell out of it. Sparks shot toward the watching bucks. Once more Yellow Snake moved a foot, and then another, until he was no more than a yard from Gallagher, and the carbine in his hands was almost touching Gallagher's broad back.

"Zastee," said Yellow Snake coldly.

"Kill and be damned to ye," said Gallagher.

Gallagher dropped the shoe into the forge, picked up

THE BORDER GUIDON 63

another one with the tongs, placed it onto the anvil, and began to shape it. He began to count as he struck hard at the shoe. "One! Two! Three! Four! Shut the door! Five! Six! Seven! Eight! I wish to hell I had closed the gate!"

"Zastee!" said the Apache a little louder.

The girl had placed her hands flat against the back wall of the shop, and now she swayed a little from side to side until Gallagher steadied her with a glance.

Yellow Snake came a little closer to Gallagher; the cold ring of the carbine muzzle touching the sweating flesh just above the kidneys.

Gallagher wiped the sweat from his face and resumed work.

The big hammer of the carbine was thumbed back with a click-cluck sound. *"Zastee! Zastee!"* said the warrior.

The others stood there, a faint look of fear on their broad faces. The sparks showered toward them, and they moved back a little.

Gallagher took another shoe from the forge and began to beat time as he sang:

> "Oh, the dragoon bold! He scorns all care,
> As he goes the rounds with uncropped hair;
> He spends no thought on the evil star
> That sent him away to the border war!"

The chief would have to crowd past Gallagher to reach the woman, and it would take a lot of crowding to move that muscular one hundred and ninety pounds. Yellow Snake looked up at Gallagher. The Irishman brought the hammer down hard so that the hot sparks danced against the warrior's naked chest, but Klij-Litzogue did not wince or speak. Once again the eyes clashed like crossing blades. Then the Apache looked at the woman. He crooked a finger at her in silent command to come to him. She did not move. Her hands were behind her, holding the pistol. Was it now? Should she shoot herself quickly, before he reached her and before the rest of them swarmed over the mad Irishman who shaped horseshoes in front of a bloodthirsty audience as though they did not exist? *Now?* Her hand tightened on the gun butt slippery with sweat.

Gallagher snatched another glowing shoe from the forge, slapped it down on the anvil, and began a frenzied beating on it so that the station rang with the sound and sparks showered the interior of the little shop. The warriors drew back, covering their mouths with their hands in awe. Yellow Snake tried once more to get past Gallagher, but this time a glowing shoe was held up in the tongs a foot from his naked chest, and even an Apache couldn't ignore that! His eyes widened. He glanced at the woman he wanted, then back at the huge Irishman. Then he spat full in Gallagher's face.

Gallagher dropped the hammer from his right hand, badly as he wanted to crack the Apache's skull with it. He doubled a huge freckled fist, and the blow traveled short and true, catching Yellow Snake flush on the jaw, lifting him from his feet and driving him back against his mates.

Gallagher wasted no time. He snatched a shoe from the fire and advanced toward the wide-eyed bucks. "*Ugashe! Ugashe!* Go! Go!" he yelled at the top of his voice, brandishing the glowing shoe in their very faces.

"*Pesh-chidin!*" one of them cried. He turned and fled, followed by the others. "*Pesh-chidin! Pesh-chidin!*"

Gallagher dropped the shoe into the forge, wiped the sweat and spittle from his face, gripped Yellow Snake by the heels, and dragged him outside. He looked at the backs of the warriors as they ran toward the gateway. Then he looked down at the unconscious chief. The devil in Gallagher wanted him to strip the bastard naked and throw him out on the ground beyond the gate, but there would be hell to pay and no pitch hot if he did. He gripped the warrior by the heels and hauled him to the gateway, then he propped him against the outer wall, wiped his hands on his trousers, and walked back to the shop.

The girl was gone. Where? . . . Then he saw her. She had fallen in a dead faint behind a work bench. He bathed her face, but she did not move. Her breasts rose and fell, and her body was warm and soft in his thick arms. He clumsily brushed her dark hair back from her

I Am Going To Send You A Personally Selected Sample Import-FREE!

...and I'll tell you exactly how to turn it into big money! Coupon brings your sample import and facts about

24,221 Money Making Products to start you in your own fabulous BIG PROFIT HOME IMPORT BUSINESS

MY PLAN STARTS YOU FAST...Shows How To

Buy Below Wholesale

how to deal direct and cut out costly middlemen so you keep all the profits!

MEN—WOMEN...get fast start without product investment. My Plan guides your every step. Your age, location, past experience not important. Imports offer profits beyond your wildest dreams. Membership in International Traders free of charge, puts you in direct contact with suppliers abroad. The sample I send you FREE is typical of my dazzling, profit-making discoveries. No obligation. No salesman will call. Rush card today.

B. L. Mellinger — Famous World Trader, internationally known Mail Order Export President, The Mellinger Co. "I started a few years ago in my garage, with less than $100. Today my business spans the globe. I will help YOU in succeeding, using my experience. Mail card!"

Surplus JEEP $812. F.O.B. Germany Running Like New!

Surplus English MOTORCYCLE 350 CC Low Mileage $170. F.O.B. England

Tiger Eye Ring $3.50

SAVE ON PERSONAL PURCHASES TOO!

BUY ONE AT A TIME OR BUY IN QUANTITY

Many of these 24,221 imports you can buy one at a time...others you can order in quantity, with minimum total order as low as 100 Jade Necklace only $3.95. Other examples, 100 Electric Razors only $2.68 ea. or 25 for $2.98 ea. One Mink Coat $385 for $6.95 ea. Electronic tested Digital Watch $7.76 ea. or 100 for $6.95 ea. All these prices include duty and shipping. Cut out U.S. middlemen. Buy below wholesale. Deal the International Traders way!

Mail Card for Free Report and Sample Import Free!

Electric Razor $3.69

Mink Coat $385.

French Perfume $1.60

Aluminum Tennis Racket $3.95

Digital Watch $6.95

S. American Poncho you make 52% profit.

10 Speed Bike $39.

Jade Necklace $2.95

Inflatable Boat $4.80

Metal Detector $2.75

This Certificate Good for

ONE SAMPLE IMPORT - FREE

B. L. Mellinger/The Mellinger Co., Dept. A178C
6100 Variel Ave., Woodland Hills, CA 91364

Send FREE REPORT, "How to Import and Export." Show how I can start a business of my own. I understand there is no obligation and no salesman will call. (If under 21, state age).

Name _____ Age ____
Address _____
City _____ State ____ Zip _____

Save 3 days — Give Zip for Fast Reply

IMPORTANT I agree to limit my request to only one Free Sample Import. I have not previously requested this Free Sample. I am 18 years or older. Initial here ____

BUSINESS REPLY MAIL
NO POSTAGE STAMP NECESSARY IF MAILED IN THE UNITED STATES

— POSTAGE WILL BE PAID BY —

The Mellinger Co.

6100 Variel Avenue

Woodland Hills, Ca. 91364

Dept. A178C

FIRST CLASS
PERMIT 402
Woodland Hills, Calif.

FREE! 164 PAGES OF TERRIFIC BARGAINS
SEND FOR OUR
GIANT CATALOG
containing over 4500 unique buys in

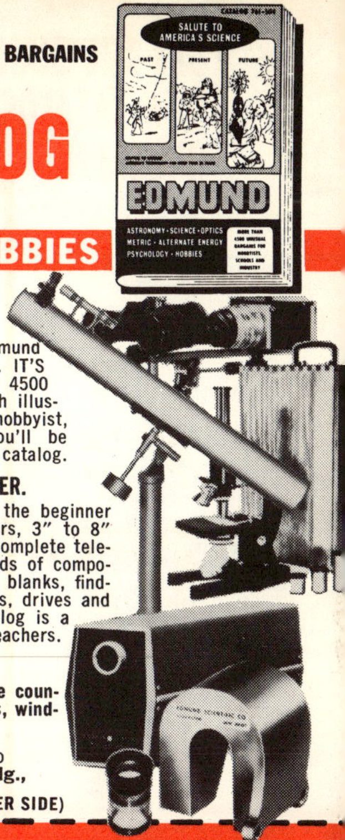

OPTICS • SCIENCE • HOBBIES

for experimenters, hobbyists, do-it-yourselfers, schools, industrials.

Don't miss this gold mine of information from Edmund Scientific Co., America's greatest science mart. IT'S FREE! 164 easy-to-read pages packed with over 4500 exciting and hard-to-get bargains, crammed with illustrations, charts, diagrams. Whether you're a hobbyist, experimenter, do-it-yourselfer or educator, you'll be amazed at the rare, low-cost buys in this giant catalog.

BIG SAVINGS FOR THE AMATEUR ASTRONOMER.
Complete range of astronomical telescopes for the beginner to the serious amateur. Reflectors and refractors, 3" to 8" from $49.95 to $895.00. Or build one yourself. Complete telescope kits, grinding and polishing kits, thousands of components and accessories including: mirrors, mirror blanks, finders, eyepieces, tubes, mounts, tripods, pedestals, drives and cameras for astrophotography. The Edmund catalog is a virtual 'science fair' for junior scientists and teachers.

WE'RE ALTERNATE ENERGY HEADQUARTERS!
Solar and other alternate energy sources include country's largest assortment of solar cells and panels, windmill generators, Methane and more.

If card is missing, write for FREE CATALOG "FD" to
EDMUND SCIENTIFIC CO., 300 Edscorp Bldg., Barrington, N. J. 08007.
(SEE OTHER SIDE)

TEAR OUT, COMPLETE & MAIL THIS POSTAGE-FREE CARD NOW.

Send me the **GIANT FREE 164-PAGE EDMUND CATALOG "FD"**

EVERY ITEM (OVER 4500) SOLD WITH A 30-DAY MONEY-BACK GUARANTEE. NO SALESMAN WILL CALL.

BankAmericard
master charge THE INTERBANK CARD

Name_____

Address_____

City_____ State_____ Zip_____

GET THE GIANT EDMUND SCIENTIFIC CO. NEW CATALOG FREE! OVER 4500 UNUSUAL BARGAINS... SOMETHING FOR EVERYONE.

SHOP AND SAVE THE EDMUND WAY.

It's easy to find what you want and easy to buy, using the 164-page Edmund catalog. There's a quick, handy reference guide in front, a complete alphabetical index in back. No middleman's commissions to inflate prices, no salesman to annoy you. Browse through the catalog and order direct from your home, office, classroom or plant as easily as you mail a letter. 95% of all orders usually shipped within 72 hours . . . mostly postpaid!

THOUSANDS OF BARGAINS FOR THE HOBBYIST.

Kits, instruments and hard-to-find items to delight every hobbyist and do-it-yourselfer, all at huge savings. Surplus. Imported. American made. Kirlian photography kits. Miniature water pumps, motors, magnets, crystal growing kits, measuring magnifiers, aerial cameras, fiber optics, miniature socket and tap wrenches, high intensity lamps and many, many more. Something for the entire family.

HARD-TO-FIND BUYS FOR INDUSTRY AND RESEARCH LABS.

A treasure house of optical and scientific components to check, measure, speed work, improve quality, cut production costs. Hard-to-get surplus bargains; ingenious scientific tools — imported, domestic. Thousands of components; lenses, prisms, wedges, mirrors, mounts, accessories of all descriptions. Biofeedback monitors, biorhythm kit, dozens of instruments, magnifiers, computers, microscopes, telescopes, binoculars, infrared equipment, photo attachments. A bonanza for labs, engineers, experimenters.

SATISFACTION GUARANTEED OR MONEY BACK.

Edmund Scientific Co. guarantees complete satisfaction with every item or return in 30 days and your money is refunded. If you haven't filled out the coupon on the other side of this card, go back and do it now.

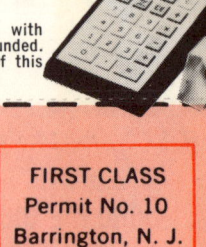

FIRST CLASS
Permit No. 10
Barrington, N. J.

BUSINESS REPLY MAIL
No postage necessary if mailed in the U.S.

Postage will be paid by

EDMUND SCIENTIFIC CO.
Dept. "FD", 300 Edscorp Building
Barrington, New Jersey 08007

Be a LOCKSMITH

Train at home—earn while you learn

LOCKSMITHING has been called "the neglected profession"—the use of locks has increased by the millions, the training of locksmiths hardly at all. The shortage is critical. The demand is fantastic.

BIG PAY JOBS WAITING. Opportunities for big cash earnings in spare time are crying for trained men everywhere. Becoming owner of your business, running your own independent shop is the logical result. And now, regardless of your age, your education, or even minor physical handicap, you can gain professional recognition in a business that is more like a hobby than like work.

IF YOU CAN READ and write we can train you. Our instruction methods have passed the rigid requirement of the New Jersey State Board of Education. The men we train and graduate are meeting with quick success. The statements of a few of them are shown on the other side of this page.

SEE FOR YOURSELF the list of more than 300 parts, tools, and pieces we furnish with the course. This includes files, tweezers, cylinders, door handles, assemblies, gauges, pins, springs, extractors, lock picks, wrench, and different kinds of locks and keys. Right from the beginning you get practical experience doing real jobs.

O.K.-prove to me

that with Locksmithing Institute training I can learn at home at my own pace. (85% of students earn money as they learn and many pay for the course with money they earn.)

NO CHARGE—NO OBLIGATION. And, no salesman will call. Send your name and we will mail—postage prepaid—our big book of facts, plus sample lesson pages. Within six weeks you can be making spare time money on preliminary jobs. Within six months you can be launched on the road to complete independence of bosses, time-clocks, lay-offs. You can open the door to a business of your own—at big money—and you can start in spare time without risking your present job.

SEND YOUR NAME TODAY. You don't even need a stamp. We pay postage on the card below when it is received at our office. Mail it today. And check the square if you are eligible for Veteran's Benefits.

306 pieces of equipment LOCKS, PICKS & TOOLS supplied for use with course, including key machine

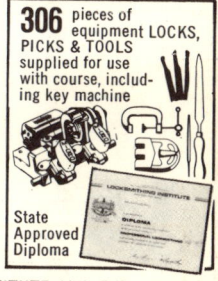

State Approved Diploma

MAIL FREE POSTCARD NOW!

FREE!

Your Opportunities in Locksmithing

LOCKSMITHING INSTITUTE, Little Falls, N.J. 07424

LICENSED BY STATE OF NEW JERSEY. ACCREDITED MEMBER NATIONAL HOME STUDY COUNCIL. APPROVED FOR VETERANS.

Please mail without obligation and postage prepaid, the FREE booklet "YOUR OPPORTUNITIES IN LOCKSMITHING", and sample lesson pages. No salesman is to call. After reading I will let you know if I am interested.

Name_____

Address_____

City_____ State & Zip_____

☐ Check here for information on Veteran Benefits.

Dept. 1262-105CD

the key — to a great future!
LOCKSMITHING SKILLS
as they were for...

I earned $1,000 while training. *Jose F. Collazo, El Paso, Texas*	Locksmithing course is well worth the tuition. *Frank R. Bishop, Holt, Mich.*
Now make $25-$30 more a week part-time! *E. Simmons-El, Bronx, N.Y.*	I'm constructing a building for my shop. *Bert DeMott, Clio, Mich.*

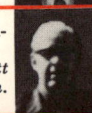

MAIL POSTAGE PAID CARD FOR FREE INFORMATION!

MAIL FREE POSTCARD NOW!

BUSINESS REPLY MAIL
No Postage Stamp Necessary If Mailed in the United States

POSTAGE WILL BE PAID BY

LOCKSMITHING INSTITUTE
A Division of Technical Home Study Schools
Little Falls, New Jersey 07424

First Class
Permit Number 137
Little Falls, N.J.

for TALL and BIG ACTIVE men

SPORTSWEAR THAT FITS

If you're a Tall or Big Guy who wants to spend Saturday on your favorite golf course, instead of trudging thru stores searching for clothes in your hard-to-find size . . . you should see the new KING-SIZE® Co. Catalog. Here are 88 pages of brand name ARROW, KING-SIZE®, McGREGOR, JANTZEN, and HUSH PUPPIES Sportswear Designed, Proportioned, and Guaranteed To Fit Tall and Big Men. New Leisure Suits and Jean Sets in Tall and Big sizes to 60; Golf and Tennis Shirts to XXL; Golf Shoes, Sneakers, and Deck Shoes to EEE . . . plus hundreds of other items for Tall & Big Men for dress or casual wear. Every item is Fully Guaranteed by the KING-SIZE® Co.

FREE CATALOG

SEND FOR FREE King-Size Co. CATALOG

Name _____
Address _____
City _____
State _____ Zip _____

BUSINESS REPLY MAIL

No postage necessary if mailed in the United States

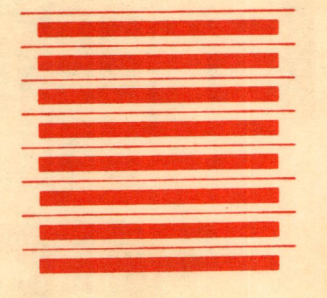

— Postage Will Be Paid By —

THE king-size CO.®

King-Size Building
Brockton, Massachusetts 02402

FIRST CLASS
PERMIT NO. 2290
BROCKTON, MASS.

pale face. She opened her eyes. "I don't understand it," she murmured.

He picked her up easily and placed her on the bench. Then he grinned. "It was a colossal bluff," he said. "They look on blacksmiths as being allied to spirits. The witch, or ghost of iron, I expect. . . . *Pesh-chidin.*"

Her face was as pale as a lily. "That face of his. Like a devil peering through the smoke of hell itself."

"Aye! Ye have a way with the words. Ye are sure ye are not Irish?"

She smiled wanly. "My grandfather was North Irish."

His face fell a little. "An Orangeman? Ah well, it cannot be helped, and even an Orangeman is an Irishman in a *sense*." He grinned. "But it was close when he spat in me face."

She nodded. "That was when I fainted. I think I hit the floor just as he did."

Gallagher ruefully eyed his big freckled fist. "Ah," he said quietly, "if I had him alone. . . . But then it would be no fun. Say two of them, or perhaps three, with no knives and no holds barred. 'Twould be a real Donnybrook!"

"What happens now?"

He shrugged. "I do not know."

"Will they be back?"

"Not likely. For a time at least. In that time we must get ready to leave."

"To go out there?"

"There is no other place to go, and we cannot stay, lass. Tonight, when it is dark, before the rising of the moon, we'll pull out of here. Do ye go now and find food and canteens. Round up any weapons ye can. Meanwhile, now that I have no audience, so to speak, I'll shoe me bay."

She placed a hand on his naked shoulder and stepped down to the floor. For a moment she looked up into his face, then she took his head between her hands, bent it forward gently, and placed her soft lips against his cracked ones. Then she was gone, leaving a faint trace of her scent behind her while he slowly touched his lips with thick fingers. "What a lass," he said. He looked at the bay. "Shannon! Ye're to be shoed! We've got to get the lass to California."

The bay looked at him quizzically.

Gallagher threw up his hands. "How do *I* know what will happen then, ye great booby?"

Chapter 8

THE SUN was dying in the west, leaving a great wash of rose and gold against the sky. Dan Gallagher smoothed the last of the graves he had dug and filled. He had not let Ellen see the body of her sister despite her pleading. He wiped the sweat from his naked torso with a huck towel. The day was almost gone. A cool wind swept through the bosque, rustling the leaves. It would be cold that night.

They had not come back, or at least he had seen no signs of them. But Klij-Litzogue would never forget Dan Gallagher as long as he lived. He would thirst for his vengeance, and it would be a terrible and bloody thing if he achieved it.

He picked up the spade and walked toward the buildings. The bay was saddled and loaded with cantle and pommel packs, an extra carbine, and half a dozen canteens. The guidon had been thrust into its socket and the arm strap tied to the saddle. It fluttered in the breeze, seemingly anxious to get back to the regiment where it belonged. Gallagher swung up the spade in a saber salute as he passed it.

She was waiting for him dressed in male clothing that had probably belonged to the boy who had been killed. The gunbelt about her slim waist was weighted down by the Colt he had given her. She had cut her hair shorter and had tied it at the nape of her neck with a bright-yellow ribbon. She wore a low-crowned, flat-brimmed hat. "How do I look?" she asked.

"Fine. But the ribbon is the wrong color."

"So?"

He placed a finger on the orange stripe alongside his blue trousers. "The dragoon color, although it pains an

Irishman such as meself, is orange. The cavalry wear yellow, and the mounted rifles wear the blessed green."

She flushed a little. "I wasn't thinking of the dragoons, Sergeant, when I tied my hair."

It was his turn to flush. "They are buried," he said to cover up his confusion. "Is it in yer mind to say a few words over them?"

"No. I can't do it, Sergeant.

"Then I will. Come."

She glanced at him curiously as he led the way to the graves. There were many unusual facets to the character of this big rough man, and they constantly surprised her.

Gallagher picked up his undershirt and jacket and put them on, then removed his disreputable hat and bowed his head. For a moment he stood there, as though groping for words, and then he spoke in a soft fine voice that was almost in direct contrast to his usual sharpness of speech: *"The Lord is my shepherd; I shall not want. He maketh me to lie down in green pastures: he leadeth me beside the still waters. . ."*

When he had finished it was dark and the wind was stronger.

"Do you soldiers always do such things?" she asked quietly.

He placed his hat upon his head and looked off into the unseen distance, almost as though he were eying other times and other places unknown to her. "Over the graves of many comrades. The lonely resting-places scattered in Utah and in Texas; in New Mexico and Arizona. Perhaps *they* do not hear it, but it gives the rest of us who are still living a little comfort." He turned quickly and walked away from the graves.

When she was alone she realized he had left her to be with her sister. She knelt beside the mound, said a quiet prayer, passed a soft hand across the grave, then got quickly to her feet and walked toward the big man who seemed to be all she had left.

He led the way from the quiet place. The water bubbled up steadily in the pool. A shutter banged in the rising wind. The black patches where the blood had soaked into the thirsty caliche showed up dimly in the darkness.

They did not look back as they passed from the bosque into the open plain. The wind snapped out the guidon. Gallagher looked ahead as he walked. Fort Coulter was to the southwest to the best of his recollection. He could have found it easily enough following the stage route, then the wagon road, then cutting off through a little-known pass in the Diablos. But now he wasn't so sure. Fortunately, God had fashioned a built-in compass in his brain, and many a time on forced marches in the old days, when everyone was a little panicky with the fear of being lost in unknown country, Gallagher had led the way with the true instinct of a homing pigeon.

It was the girl who worried him. There was no going back for Gallagher. He would cast the dice the hard way and live or die depending upon which way the ivory cubes fell. He would not cry out if he lost. That was not the way of a dragoon. But for her he felt a twinge of his deep-seated pity. She was strong, but not strong enough for what lay ahead of them. Few women, and not too many men, could live in that country even in times of peace. During war, especially against the Apaches, it was only the toughest fighters who survived.

Yet he felt better for having her with him. He knew he was a fool. She'd never live to see the Stars and Stripes snapping in a fresh breeze over a post of the United States Army. One way or another she would have to die, and the way of dying would be hard indeed. By thirst or by weakness; by hand of Apache or perhaps her own hand. Perhaps, and this was the worst thought of all, it would have to be by *his* hand.

"Supposing she comes back to the place?" she asked out of the darkness.

He glanced at her dim face.

"I mean Judith, Dan."

They strode on for fifty yards.

"Dan?"

He looked away from her. "She will not be coming back, lass," he said in a low voice.

The moon washed the country in silver light, etching sharp shadows upon the harsh earth. Now and then Gallagher looked back. There had been no sign of them since the two had left the buildings. It was odd and a little bit eerie, plodding across the moon-washed ground, like silhouettes in a shadow theater, easily seen from a mile or two away, and yet nothing else moved in the cold bright moonlight.

"Will they follow us?" she asked.

"Yes."

She looked back over a slim shoulder. "I don't see any of them," she said.

"That is the time to expect them, Ellen."

"What is ahead of us?"

"The Diablos. They are half hills and half mountains."

"What is beyond them?"

"To the south is Mexico; to the west, a long way off, is the Colorado."

"And to the east?"

He hesitated. "Apache country."

"But isn't this all Apache country?"

"In a way. But they have strongholds just as we have forts."

"Whose stronghold is closest?"

"Klij-Litzogue . . . Yellow Snake . . . the one who tried to get to ye in the blacksmith shop."

She made a disagreeable sound. "He must hate you for what you did."

He shrugged. "He hated me long before that." He eyed her. "This man Dunlap. Ye are sure he planned to take ye to Fort Coulter?"

"That is what he said."

"Tell me: Did he have any features a man would remember well after having seen him once?"

She was silent for a little while, then said, "It was his eyes, I think. One could never forget them. He was like one of the prophets of old at times. He knew the Bible from cover to cover, it seemed."

Gallagher glanced quickly at her. "What was his first name?"

"I can't remember. Everyone called him *Mister* Dunlap. It was a name of biblical times, I think."

"Like Elijah?"

She smiled. "Yes! That was it! Elijah Dunlap!"

A strange cold feeling crept over Gallagher.

"Did you know him, Sergeant?"

"I think so."

How could he tell her of Elijah Darris, for that was the man he was sure. Elijah Darris. Jackleg preacher. Member of some little-known and almighty strange religious sect. A man who had been driven from more civilized areas because of the unholy practices in which he delighted. A man who gave allegiance to no recognized creed and no country, only allegiance to himself and his strange perverted tastes. One of those tastes had been for women, particularly young girls.

"What do you know about him?" she asked.

"Very little." He had to lie to her. If Judith had been killed or captured by the Apaches her fate would be easier in a sense than it would be in the rough hands of Elijah Darris. There were other stories about the man, of his dealings with the Apaches; one of his friends had been none other than Klij-Litzogue.

Gallagher eyed the clear sky against which the moon hung like a silver salver. He glanced back along the way they had come. He thought he saw a faint quick movement, but then all was devoid of life again. They were back there, all right, and on each flank, and in all probability some of them had forged easily ahead to complete the ring about them. They would close in when the time was right, like howling wolves in the wild steppe country of Russia closing in on a sleigh drawn by tiring horses.

"I think she is still alive," Ellen said suddenly.

"Judith?"

"Yes."

"Why do you think so?"

She tilted her head to one side. "Because Judy has a way of doing things just like that."

"This is not a game they play out here."

"I know."

"If she is in their hands it would be better if she had died as Evelyn did."

She wrapped her arms about her shapely knees. "Judy likes men," she said thoughtfully.

"They are not such men as she might have known."

"She has known rough men. On the ship coming to California. On the stagecoaches to Los Angeles. Other places."

Gallagher looked back over his shoulder. There was something puzzling about this trip. The Apaches could have kept them penned up at the station, yet they had let them leave. Klij-Litzogue must have his revenge. If he did not he would lose face amongst his people, and they had no place in their stern way of life for such a leader or such a man.

Somewhere to the south a coyote howled softly. A moment later the call was answered by another coyote far to the north. Gallagher raised his head. The call came again, this time from the east. Ellen shivered. "They sound so lonely," she said.

"Yes."

The fourth and last call came as he had expected it to, from the west, and it sent the cold sweat trickling down his sides. There was no advantage in telling the girl that those were not coyotes out there, but Apaches, and that they had completely surrounded Gallagher and her with an unseen and deadly escort.

Chapter 9

It was just before the false dawn when Gallagher stopped walking and looked at Ellen. "There is something I must do," he said quietly, "and ye must help me."

Her face was dim in the faint light. His heart went out to her, for he knew she was badly frightened. "What is it, Dan?" At least her voice was steady. She had good control.

"I am going back to bleed them a little."

"I don't understand."

He drew her close. "It is better to outflank an advancing enemy than a retreating one. I am going back. Ye will go on, for they will hear the horse. It will not be easy for ye to be alone in the darkness, knowing they are close, but it is close to the dawn, and they might jump us then. They will not expect me, Ellen." He smiled wryly. "At least I hope not."

"And I'm to be the bait."

"Aye."

He was as ready as he'd ever be, with Sharps carbine, twin issue Colts, and a long-bladed bowie, which was not issue, but few veteran Indian-fighters were without one of the heavy-bladed gutters. "Ellen," he said quietly.

"You don't have to tell me, Dan. I have the pistol ready." She smiled wanly. "If anything happens to you I'll take the guidon back to where it rightfully belongs. With the First Dragoons."

"That's the dragoon spirit!" He lowered his voice. "Do not be afraid if ye hear shooting. I hope it will be *my* shooting. Now go on, traveling at the same pace we have kept up all night."

She placed a cool hand against his rough cheek and

touched her lips against his. "Good luck, dragoon," she said, and suddenly she was gone into the dimness.

Gallagher removed his spurs and placed them in a pocket. He padded back with carbine at hip level. His eyes darted back and forth, eying and evaluating each shadow, each faint movement. Then he saw the place—a low swale rimmed with thorny brush. To the left of it, fifty yards away, was a low mound of rock that thrust itself up above the flat ground like an angry boil ready for eruption. To the right was a low ledge that extended for about two hundred yards. To the northeast the ground sloped down, and it was almost barren of brush.

He entered the swale and removed his hat, letting it drop onto his back, hanging by the strap. He took out one of his Navy Colts, cocked it, and placed it on a flat rock near at hand. Now there was nothing to do but wait . . . and think.

They might expect an ambush. They were tophole fighters themselves, masters of the unseen ambush, the spit of a rifle from concealment. Just as they were masters of the ambush, they also feared it more than any other form of attack. It was logical for them to be on the lookout for an ambush near the low mound to Gallagher's left. At least he hoped so. The mound unconsciously drew the eye on that flat plain.

They were in sight before he realized how quickly they were moving—seven of them, mounted on their ponies, following the unseen trail to pass between mound and swale. Gallagher wet his dry lips. Seven of them. He had thirteen rounds between carbine and two pistols. Twelve of those rounds were in the Colts, hardly a weapon for long-range or even middle-range shooting. Then, too, there would be more warriors within earshot.

She would be moving on, trending to the southwest. What if he was killed or captured? She would go on then until they showed up silently waiting for her. She might put up a fight, but it would not be for long, and then they would have her, and she would die by her own hand.

"Ah, God," he said softly and drove the thoughts from

his teeming mind. There was work to be done. His chosen trade, fighting the enemies of his country.

Gallagher eased back the big hammer of the Sharps to full cock. He lowered his head and rested his cheek against the stock, sighting on the last rider. Closer and closer they came until the lead horseman was not more than fifty yards from Gallagher. Gallagher took in the slack of the trigger, steadied the carbine, picked up the broad chest of the brave on the knife-blade front sight, settled the front sight in the notch of the rear sight. Then he touched off the carbine.

The Sharps bucked back against his shoulder, driving a puff of smoke toward the Apaches. The slamming report of the shot seemed to roll across the flat plain. The warrior was driven back off the rump of his horse by the impact of the big .52 caliber slug.

Gallagher reloaded, lowering the breech, slipping in a linen-covered cartridge, raising the block to shear off the rear of the cartridge, capping the nipple, all in swift well-timed movements, so that when he sighted again the Apaches were still milling in confusion.

The second shot struck a yelling Apache in the left shoulder. The third knocked a buck from his horse, and the fourth round killed a horse. Then Gallagher was gone, running swiftly along the ledge, bent low so that he could not be seen, reloading as he ran, leaving a cloud of drifting smoke to mark the place where the Apaches had begun to plant lead.

Gallagher hit the ground fifty yards up the ledge, thrust the carbine forward, sighted, and squeezed off. The slug creased one of the bucks, who fell as if dead. The lead Apache screamed as he jerked his lance from its sling, couched it, and raced toward Gallagher, who was reloading.

"Trying to make a bloody hero out of yerself, is it?" grunted Gallagher.

He raised the carbine and sighted. The chest of the buck got bigger and bigger, and then Gallagher pulled the trigger. The Sharps misfired. There was no time to reload. Gallagher jumped to his feet and jerked out his

Colt. The lance was ten feet from his chest when he fired twice, then dived over the ledge and rolled away. The lance blade drove into the ground inches away from Gallagher. The warrior was pitchforked from his horse, landing with a dull thud a few feet from his quarry. He raised his head, and then dropped it as Gallagher's knife sank in deep, probed for the heart, and drove in another inch or two.

Gallagher reloaded his Sharps and gripped the dead buck's pony by the hackamore. He swung up into the rough saddle. The pony reared and fought viciously, but a hard blow atop the head from the steel-shod butt of the carbine brought him around. Gallagher slammed the carbine barrel against the flanks of the pony and rode like a fury, to the west, but as he turned to look back he saw the face of the buck he had dismounted by killing his horse. It was the face of Yellow Snake.

"*Zastee! Zastee!* Kill! Kill!" yelled Gallagher.

The pony's hoofs drummed on the hard earth. There was a trace of the false dawn in the eastern sky. The wind picked up. Behind Gallagher, near the low swale, lay two dead warriors, two wounded warriors, and a dead horse. The big White-eye had not only ambushed skilled ambushers but had added insult to injury by stealing an Apache horse right under the noses of Yellow Snake and his best men.

She was waiting near an upthrust shoulder of rock, the pistol in her hand. She raised it as she saw the lone horseman bearing down on her, then lowered it again. No Apache was *that* big."

He slid from the horse. "Mount!" he snapped, jerking his thumb toward the bay. "We can get a good lead on them now. They will not be anxious to close in." He slung the carbine over his shoulder and fought to get the excited Apache horse under control until at last he brought a huge fist down atop the head of the horse. It seemed to the girl that the legs of the horse wobbled a little from the effect of the blow.

They rode to the southwest as the light grew, and there was no sign of the enemy. She looked at him as she guided the bay past broken ground. "Have you nothing to say?" she demanded at last.

He looked at her in surprise. "What do ye mean?"

"What happened back there?"

He grinned reminiscently. "It was a fine fight. A bit onesided, ye might say, what with one Irishman against the seven of them."

She paled. "Seven of them?"

"The odds were a little on my side, lass."

"But you are not marked!"

He waved a hand. "They never had a chance to mark me, Ellen."

Then he thought back on that hot little fight . . . the misfiring of the Sharps and the lance attack of the warrior. It had been a close thing. The reaction from it made his stomach roll over within him. It had been too damned close for comfort.

"To the right," he said.

She guided the bay closer to his mount.

"See the dark line against the earth? That is a draw, or an arroyo, and we can shelter there. God help us if they have gotten there first!"

They reached the lip of the draw as the sky lightened fully with the dawn. Gallagher whistled softly. The draw seemed to drop into the very bowels of the earth. It was deep and not very wide, fifty yards at the most. Gallagher looked back over his shoulder. "Into it, lass!" he ordered. She hesitated. He drove the horse at it, leaning forward as it slid down the steep decline in a shower of gravel and stones. He could not see the bottom. Perhaps it was a sheer drop after a time, but if it was it was too damned late, for Gallagher was on his way down.

The girl followed him, riding the big bay easily, but her heart was in her mouth as she saw Gallagher's broad back vanish into the darkness below her. She could hear the rocks rumbling past her, loosened by her descent. Dust billowed up, choking her.

Then she saw him standing beside his horse, holding its head and looking up at her with drawn face. He caught the bay by the mane as it reached the place beside him. "Do not look down!" he said to her.

But she couldn't help it. They stood on a narrow ledge, hardly more than eight feet wide, beyond which there was nothing, a sheer drop into blackness. She closed her eyes and swayed in the saddle, feeling his arms about her as he helped her down. "We must move on," he said.

"Let's rest. I'm frightened, Gallagher."

"Get on with ye! There is no time to waste! We have been lucky so far! Get on with ye!"

She stumbled along the ledge ahead of him. He looked down into the chasm they had almost fallen into. "Jesus," he said softly as he led the two horses on after Ellen.

The light of day filled the canyon. The ledge was wider now, and it sloped downward, but still the bottom of the chasm on the right was a long way down.

Gallagher could see that the girl was almost exhausted. Once again he looked over his shoulder for signs of pursuit. It would have been easy for them to roll rocks over the brink high above the two white people, like playing a deadly game of skittles. But there was no sign of them. A hawk hovered high overhead, almost at ground level with the lip of the canyon. He did not seem afraid, almost sure sign that there was no human life up there.

It was strange, but then there had been a number of strange things about the journey he and the girl had made from the station. It would have been easy for the Indians to pen the two whites in the station, or to cut them off on the open plain; finally, they could have followed the lip of the canyon, knowing well enough they had their quarry in a great natural prison.

Gallagher looked ahead. There seemed to be no way out of the place, yet there might be unseen openings that led up to the ground level to the east. There had better be . . .

They reached the bottom of the canyon. Ellen Eustis turned. "Look," she said quietly.

Ahead of them, beneath a great rock overhang, were *tinajas,* rock pans of water filled by seepage from some hidden source. The water rippled in the cool morning wind of the canyon. Shannon whinnied. Gallagher held onto the horses and looked about. The place was as dead as an Egyptian tomb. Not a sign of life. The brush and scrub trees moved uneasily in the wind. Gallagher looked above them. Nothing but the jagged rimrock and the blue sky, dotted with a few hurrying clouds.

He shook his head as he led the horses to the water and let them drink their fill. It was almost as though they had wandered off the earth to some unknown and deserted planet.

They made their camp up a talus slope, in a deep cave protected by great fallen rocks. There was a seepage of water at the rear of the cave—enough to keep them alive for days if they were besieged in the cave.

She dropped onto the blanket he had spread for her and fell asleep almost immediately.

Gallagher had led the horses into the cave. He rubbed them down and let them feed on dried grasses he had pulled. He walked to the mouth of the cave and looked out across the peaceful sunlit canyon. It was a nice place. Quiet and peaceful looking. Far to his right, almost due south, it seemed as though the canyon widened and formed a vast Y, and he could have sworn he saw sunlight sparkling on running water.

On the far wall of the canyon he saw a rather even line, a fault perhaps, with a curiously irregular pattern of light and dark rock. He stared at it and then struck his right fist into his left palm. "By God," he said. "I wouldn't have believed it! This must be Canyon Encantado! There is no other place like it in this country. And if it is Canyon Encantado, then we are safe from the Apaches, for the place is taboo to them!"

He rubbed his bristly jaws. It was sheer good fortune. They would be safe enough in there . . . for a time at least. Some time soon they would have to leave it if Gallagher carried on with his mission. His face tightened. The mission! There would be a reception committee awaiting them when they left the canyon. Men with thick black manes of hair and greasy tearing hands holding hard-edged knives ready for soft white-eye flesh.

▶▶ Chapter 10

THE GREAT canyon was filled with the sun and warmth of midday. A fitful breeze felt its way along the canyon and rustled the foliage. Dan Gallagher awoke with a start. He glanced at Ellen, who was still asleep. He cursed himself softly as he gathered his weapons. If it was not Canyon Encantado the Tontos might have crept up on the two of them.

He walked to the front of the cave and stood just inside the entrance, just short of the light of the sun, eying the floor of the canyon and the far wall. It was castellated, a curious conglomeration of spires, domes, towers, and battlements. With half-closed eyes and a little imagination the formations appeared man-made, lacking only banners and men-at-arms, with their armor shining in the sunlight.

There was no sign of life. Gallagher worked his way out of the cave by crawling through a jumble of rock and brush. He lay for a long time studying the great trough of the canyon. The trail by which they had entered was but a hairline against the sheer salmon- and yellow-colored rock wall.

He eased his way down the talus lope, taking advantage of every scrap of cover and shade, until he found himself in a tangled labyrinth of rocks and brush where the going was slow but the cover was excellent. It took him an hour to reach a place where he could see the stream. It was wider than he had expected and ran between grassy banks overhung by tree branches. A rabbit moved from one patch of cover to another. A small bear prowled about a meadow.

Gallagher walked around a huge naked shoulder of rock and then stopped short. A hundred yards from him was a high-walled corral build of fieldstone. A rough track led from it toward the stream, then continued on the other side of the ford.

Dan scratched his growing beard. Indians would never have built such a corral. Peeled poles were good enough for them. It was obviously the work of white men . . . but no white men lived there! At least he had never heard of white men living there.

He squatted in the shade of a boulder and scanned the rough trail that followed the far side of the stream until it vanished into a wall of greenery that lay like a thick dam across the width of the right-hand branch of the Y.

Gallagher shrugged. He walked slowly back to the cave. Fort Coulter was about twenty miles from this place, as best as he could estimate. He'd have to go there. Taking the girl along was out of the question. This place was as good as any in which to leave her. If it was Canyon Encantado the Apaches would certainly leave her alone. But the corral was a puzzler. He looked back toward the great Y. Maybe Mormons had built it. They built well, and this was their kind of country, for they were more farmers than cattlemen or miners, but it was a long way south from their home base.

She was waiting for him inside the entrance to the cave, with gunbelt about her slim waist and the heavy carbine across her lap. "Are you sure there are no settlements around here?" she asked.

"None that I know of."

"What is this place?"

"Canyon Encantado."

She looked up at him. "Charmed Canyon?"

He squatted beside her and took up a handful of dirt in his great hands. "More likely 'Enchanted Canyon,' Ellen." He looked up at her as he let the earth fall from one hand to the other. "They tell strange stories about this place. It was the Spanish conquistadores who named it, as ye can guess. But even before their time, according to what yer father once told me"—here he looked down at his busy hands—"the Apaches shunned this place."

"But why?"

He gestured with the empty hand. "See yon rock

formation across the canyon? See the alternate lights and darks av it?"

"Yes."

"Look closely then. If ye cannot see sharply enough yer father's fine Vollmer glasses are in one av me saddlebags."

She stared at the wall, then looked strangely at him. "But it is man-made," she said wonderingly.

He nodded. "Yon great crevice is filled with fieldstone work. Room after room av them. Far back into the crevice. With windows and doors. The T-shaped openings are the doors."

"But who built them?"

He shrugged. He dropped the earth and dusted his hands. "The 'Hohokam,' I think they are called. The old ones. The people who were here long before the Apaches, it is said. They left. No one knows why. Perhaps famine, disease, lack of water, any number av reasons. But leave they did."

"Why did they live in a place like this?"

"Water. Tillable soil. Natural protection."

"Against the elements?"

He looked up at her. "Partly."

"What else would there be to be frightened off"

He stood up and looked out upon the peaceful canyon. "The same thing we came in here to get away from . . . the Apaches."

She paled a little. "Will they come after us?"

He shook his head. "But we cannot leave without running into them again. It will be like a great prison for ye until I get back."

She stood up slowly. A slim hand traveled to the white column of her throat. "What do you mean?" she faltered.

Gallagher's face grew hard. "I am not going to deceive ye, lass. I am on a mission, ordered to it by yer own father, and I must go."

"They can't expect one man to carry out such a mission! Forget about it, Dan."

"Ye will be safe here. God knows I don't want to leave ye, but I must go."

She looked up into his face. "You're a brave man, Dan Gallagher, but as big a fool as any I have ever met!" She walked away from him toward the rear of the cave.

Gallagher shrugged. It was always the way. Explaining such a thing to a female was like butting your skull against Blarney Castle. It would not give.

Gallagher went outside and eyed the canyon walls. That corral still bothered him. But they had seen no sign of life. No fresh horse or mule droppings. No Apaches, either. It was Canyon Encantado all right; it had to be!

He cocked an eye at the sun, still high in the sky. He would have to leave this evening, before the moon arose, or bide his time until it was gone and he could scale his way out of the canyon. He looked up at the great sheer walls. Here and there they had crumbled and left wide notches in the rimrock. It would not be easy for a man to scale the walls, and with a horse to get up there, too, he'd have the devil of a time of it. But he had to have a horse, and he could not leave by any of the canyon entrances. The Tontos might not have the guts to come into the place, but they had the patience and the time to wait outside for Gallagher.

All the strange stories of this fabled place came back to haunt him as he stood there. He shivered a little as the breeze slowly reversed itself to flow down canyon as it always did at nightfall. But it was more than the cool wind that made him shiver. There was *something* in that canyon besides animal life and the decaying bones of cliff-dweller structures. *Something*...

They ate in the darkness. Gallagher had lighted a candle in a niche around a curve in the cave wall long enough for her to prepare their supper, and then he had insisted on extinguishing it. She wondered why. He had said that the Tontos would not come in there no matter how badly they wanted the two of them. But she knew something was bothering him.

He busied himself after they had eaten, getting his gear ready for his trip to Fort Coulter. There was feeling of dread within her, not so much for her own safety, even though the prospect of being left there alone was frightening, but for his. They did not speak to each other, but each of them knew what the other was thinking. At least they thought they knew. Each of them individually had begun to sense an inner stirring, a feeling that had not been present until they had returned to the cave, but neither of them knew the same feeling was in the mind and soul of the other one.

"When will you leave?" she asked at last.

He sheathed one his Colt. "As soon as I saddle the bay."

She leaned against the wall of the cave, slowly letting down her damp hair to dry it. "That soon?"

"Yes. There will be darkness before the coming of the moon. By the time it is gone I will be in the open."

"But can you escape them then?"

He grinned in the darkness and patted his Sharps and one of the Colts. "I am not worried."

"But the horse. Can their ponies outrun him?"

"Shannon?" He laughed. "He is a Denmark breed, lass. Yes, ma'am, a direct descendant of old Gaines Denmark himself, he is!"

"Oh," she said vaguely.

He gathered his gear together and looked down at it in the darkness. She slowly dried her hair. "How long will you be gone?"

"Not long," he said. He walked to the rear of the cave and lighted the candle, making sure he concealed the glow of the light from the rest of the cave by hanging a blanket in front of it. He took out the dispatch that concerned his mission and read it slowly so that he could memorize the contents. Then he concealed the dispatch in a niche of the cave wall. He turned and snuffed out the candle, then dropped the blanket. As he did so he felt her close to him. "I'm afraid, Dan," she said in a little voice.

He placed his hands on her shoulders and felt the soft dampness of her hair. "Ye will be all right," he said.

"It's not for myself," she said, "but for you, Dan."

They stood there in the darkness, and then she placed her hands against the sides of his face and drew it down so that his mouth met her lips. She had kissed him before but never like this. His arms went about her and he lifted her off her feet, feeling the softness of her body against him, and he remembered her as he had first seen her in the guttering yellow light of the candle, naked and with a knife ready in her hand.

He carried her to the mouth of the cave and kissed her again. They did not speak for a long time as they sat there close together, the wind whispering softly down the canyon.

"I will be back, lass," he said at last.

She clung to him and rested her head against his shoulder.

"Ye are a soldier's daughter. Ye must know that I have to go, Ellen. It is my duty."

"Yes."

He kissed her and drew her tightly to him, and his hands felt the softness of her. Then he stood up and reached for his weapons.

"Look, Dan," she said.

He turned. There was a faint suspicion of soft silver light against the eastern sky, above the notched rimrock of the canyon. He could not leave her now; not for some hours; not until the moonlight was gone. He walked to her and drew her close.

They lay down upon the blankets and watched the silvery glory of the new moon as it rose. They talked in low voices, and Dan Gallagher knew he was deeply in love with her.

The moon traveled swiftly, it seemed to Dan, and when the cave mouth was in thick shadowy darkness he knew it would not be long before he would have to leave her. By the time he found his way out of the canyon the moon would be gone and he could travel in the darkness.

But her arms would not release him, and he felt a powerful surging within him. He had not been with a woman for a long time, far too long to be tempted like this, and she did not resist when his hands became more intimate. At last there came a time when both of them knew there could hardly be a turning back.

There was no need to talk. She was there for the taking, and he knew she would not resist. He hovered on the verge, covering her face with kisses while he fumbled with her clothing. Then he noticed that her face was wet with her tears as well as with his kisses.

"What is it, Ellen?" he asked.

She drew herself closer to him and clung to him tightly.

"Ellen?"

"Go on, Dan," she said almost fiercely.

He started again, and then he stopped. He rolled back a little and looked down at the dim loveliness of her oval face. She was ready for him, she would not resist, but something held him back. He suddenly knew why she would let him take her. He mentally tore himself away from her, kissed her gently, then stood up.

"Dan?"

"Yes?"

She hesitated. "Don't you *want* me?"

"Aye! With all my heart."

"Then?"

He gathered his gear and walked to the mouth of the cave. He stood there for a few minutes looking out in the moving shadows. He could hear her irregular breathing. She would have given herself to him because she thought she'd never see him again. But why? Because he was a man going to his death and she was sorry for him? Because she loved him and wanted a last eternal memory of him?

"Dan," she said tenderly.

He turned and walked to her. She was sitting up. He took her face in one great hand and raised it, kissing her gently, without the hot passion of before, and she knew by this token that his love for her was far deeper than even she had realized.

He walked quickly to the mouth of the cave and looked back. "Thanks," he said quietly.

"For what, Dan?"

"For ye. For yer love. For my being a man and ye being a woman. I will be back, Ellen. Nothing can stop me.

It is then that we'll know a love greater than this we know now. Goodbye, love."

Then he was gone, with hardly a sound of his passing, and she was alone, yet not alone in the darkness. For wherever she would be, and whatever might happen, she loved Dan Gallagher and knew she was loved by him. Nothing else quite seemed to matter anymore.

▶▶ *Chapter* 11

FORT Coulter, or what was left of it, was now garrisoned by the bat, the owl, the mouse, and the rattlesnake. The thought was Dan Gallagher's as he lay on his lean belly and studied the ruins through the captain's field glasses. The fine German lens seemed to draw the buildings in close, sharp and clear, under the bright morning sun. There wasn't a sign of life about the place.

Tumbleweeds were stacked in windrows against walls and in the corrals. The flagpole had been shattered and riven and now lay across the parade ground. Even the post cemetery had not been spared. The mounds had been lowered by the keening winds and the headboards driven aslant and weathered by wind and pelting rain.

Gallagher lowered the glasses. Somewhere about that post, certainly not *in* it, would be the weapons and supplies, if they had not been moved elsewhere. He rested his chin on his folded arms and studied the terrain. The rutted wagon road ran northeast, trending to Gallagher's left and by-passing the great canyon he had left the night before. To south, west, and east were rugged hills, masses of decomposing rock, stippled with scrub trees and thorny vegetation. In the whole area there was hardly enough water to wet a cricket's throstle.

Gallagher rubbed his whiskered jaws. Now that he was here he really didn't know where to start looking, but he had to start, that was sure. He walked back to the tired bay and led him down into an arroyo, where, after a watering, he picketed him. Gallagher took carbine, field glasses, and a canteen, then left the bay. Shannon *might* be there when he got back.

He worked his way through the draws and arroyos, looking for telltale signs, but found nothing of value.

He circled the entire post. Nothing. He did not want to enter the fort proper, but it had to be done. Artenis would hardly have been able to conceal the small arms, the six howitzers, and the mass of equipment within the post, but Gallagher had to see for sure.

He poked about in the buildings. They had done a good job when they had left the post. A great mass of ashes, humped with blackened iron and charred wood, lay in the middle of the parade ground. The dispensary was a stinking depository of broken medicine bottles and pots of lotion mingled with dirty bandages and other hospital items.

There was nothing of value on the post. Wanderers had conceded that fact in past months, leaving as proof of their disappointment piles of human fecal matter within the buildings.

Gallagher walked to the eastern edge of the post proper and looked toward the hills. There wasn't any place in the open where the materials could have been hidden. They must be in the hills, but that would have been dangerous, because the Tontos would have seen such activities.

Gallagher squatted and balanced on his heels. A lone hawk hung in the sky. Dotted against the sharp clear blue of the sky were small clouds, and their shadows raced across the open country ahead of them in a race that was never won and never lost.

Gallagher leaned back against the building with his carbine across his thighs. He drove the thought of Ellen from his mind. He was worried about her, but his mission came first. The sooner he accomplished it the sooner he would be able to return for her. What would happen then was in the hands of the fates.

Where in God's name could that slinking bastard Artenis have hidden those weapons and supplies? A man could spend a lifetime looking through those hills if the Apaches let him live that long.

What had Artenis said? "We can use you, Gallagher. We must pass through the country of Klij-Litzogue to get those weapons and munitions. You can guide us. You are the only man who can guide us. What do you say?"

The country of Klij-Litzogue. What had he meant by that? The whole Diablo country was the country of Klij-Litzogue. Only Fort Coulter had held him in check. The country of Klij-Litzogue. Miles and miles of rugged hills and tangled canyons, fanged mountains and barren deserts. Then Gallagher slapped his hands against the sides of his head. "Jesus God!" he said hoarsely. There was only one place those weapons would have been safe other than on a military post. *Canyon Encantado!*

Klij-Litzogue would not dare enter the canyon, but the Texas mounted rifles would, if they had managed to pass through Apache country safely. That was why Artenis had wanted Gallagher to throw in his lot with the Confederacy.

Gallagher left the fort and hurried to Shannon. He cursed himself as he pulled out the picket pin. Ellen was safe enough from the Apaches as long as she stayed in the canyon; even if the rebels found her in there Gallagher did not fear for her. But if they tried to get out of that canyon under the very noses of Klij-Litzogue and his warriors they wouldn't have a chance. If Gallagher got there in time he could guide them out of the Apache country, but he'd be damned if he'd help the rebels get out of there safely with enough weapons and munitions to sway the balance between victory and defeat for the Union on the deserts of the Southwest.

He led the bay along the arroyo, hoping to God the Apaches would not spot him before dusk. He wanted to wait until darkness; every fiber in him warned him that that was the safest course, but the black dog was upon his back and would stay there until he reached Canyon Encantado.

The moon was not up yet. Gallagher stood poised at the brink of the great darkness-filled trough of the canyon. He tested the night with his senses. There had been no sign of the Apaches as he had crossed the country to get to the canyon. Maybe they were watching the Texas mounted rifles. He grinned at the thought. What a game they were all playing in that country! It reminded him of the fights they used to have in the barracks to while away the boredom and loneliness of outpost forts. They would snuff out the lights, and each man would strike out at anyone he could hit, noncom or private, big or little, friend or enemy. There was one big difference between those fights and the one that was coming up in Canyon Encantado. This one would be to the death. Three parties feeling for each other in the darkness and the loneliness.

The rebels wanted the weapons before Gallagher could get to them. Gallagher wanted to destroy them before the rebels got them. The Apaches wanted the weapons and the horses of the Texans, and they wanted the heart's blood of Daniel Timothy Gallagher. It might yet end up in a bloodletting merry-go-round.

The moonlight touched the eastern sky with a faint promise of light to come. Gallagher looked back over his shoulder. The wind whispered through the brush. Shannon nickered softly. Gallagher closed a hand on the bay's windpipe. There was something back there in the black velvet of the night.

He led the bay slowly forward. He had cased the bay's hoofs in leather and cloth. Gallagher felt for the faint trail he had found the night before. It was pitch black beneath him. Thank God he could not see over the brink, for he knew he could not march that thread of trail if he could see what was below him.

He eased his way down on to the trail like a cautious bather wading into icy water. He was fifty feet down the dangerous way when he felt that something, or someone, was standing at the head of the trail. He looked back past the horse and for a long moment or two thought it was a boulder or perhaps some form of vegetation about the height of a man. Then he remembered there had been nothing like that when he had been up there.

He continued downward, feeling his way, his thudding heart seemingly trying to leap out of his chest. Now and then he heard the harsh pattering of gravel and small stones dropping from the brink of the trail. He looked back again—the dim something up there seemed to have grown. In the faint promise of the moonlight to come he could see the thick manes of hair and the broad deep chest and shoulders of the mountain people. But they would not follow him down. Was it because of the danger? Or because they feared ambush? Or because the dark trough below him was actually the taboo Canyon Encantado?

Gallagher went on. He heard a distant scuffling sound, and something struck the trail twenty feet behind the horse. The bay reared, and Gallagher fought him, dragging his head down with the bridle reins. "Aisy, boyo!" he pleaded.

Something struck far below him, then again and again. He knew what it was: they were rolling rocks over the brink. The rocks could go where the Tontos did not dare to go. The cold sweat poured down Gallagher's sides, and for a moment blind panic seized him, urging him to plunge down that trail which would lead him straight to hell the hard way.

The rocks seemed to pour down upon the trail, striking hard, bounding off into space, then striking again and again to shatter the decomposing rock of the canyon slopes below.

A shard struck the bay, and he whinnied sharply.

"For God's sake, Shannon!" cried Gallagher.

A rock struck just ahead of Gallagher, and fragments of it struck him like a dose of canister. He staggered with the impact. Another rock struck beside the bay. Shannon surged forward, driving Gallagher to one side, pinning him against the canyon wall. Then the bay was gone, thudding down the trail while Gallagher stood there pressed against the wall listening to the devil's cannonade of rocks crashing and splintering, bounding and rolling, awakening the canyon echoes, slamming them back and forth between the walls. Gallagher closed his eyes and for the first time since he had been a boy in Ireland he prayed with all his heart and soul.

There was no sound from the bay. Dead, perhaps, or

lying with splintered ivory bones protruding through his bleeding hide.

Gallagher at last inched his way down, with the dust of the trail coating his face and drying up his throat and nostrils. Then he was at the bottom, and the rocks were dropping farther and farther away as the Tontos moved in the opposite direction.

Shannon nickered from the darkness. Gallagher walked to him, gripped him about the neck, and buried his face in the mane. He stood there for several minutes while the sweat ran down his body and soaked his dirty trail clothing.

He led the bay toward the cave area. The moon was lighting the western wall of the canyon, but the very bottom of it was thick in whispering darkness. An uneasy feeling crept over him. There was no sound from the Tontos.

He tethered the bay to a shrubby growth, then took his carbine and lowered the breech to remove the cartridge in the chamber. He thrust in a fresh cartridge, closed the breach to shear off the end of the round, then half cocked the hammer and placed a cap on the nipple.

He walked softly up the rough talus slope toward the cave. The moonlight was already bathing the rock wall above it, although the mouth of the cave was hardly more than a darker patch against the shadowed wall. He looked back. The canyon was quiet except for the ceaseless rushing of the wind.

He reached the wall and stood there listening. Nothing. Gallagher walked softly toward the cave mouth and waited again. There was no sound or sight of the girl. He walked to the entrance and whistled softly the dragoon song. She must be sleeping soundly.

He walked into the cave and leaned his head forward, trying to probe through the darkness. Ellen," he said softly.

"Ellen?"

A mouse or some other small creature scurried for cover over his feet.

"Ellen?"

Nothing.

Gallagher walked to the rear of the cave, past the turn in the wall. The place was as empty as last night's whiskey bottle.

Maybe she was playing with him.

"Ellen!"

There was nothing but the soft rushing of the wind past the cave entrance.

It was the same in the area outside of the cave. The Apache horse was gone, too. Everything was gone except the sweet memory of her and of how she had lain in his arms the night he had left, willing to let him have her body as well as her soul.

He cursed himself blackly with all the inborn skill of an imaginative race for having left her there at all.

Chapter 12

THE GREAT canyon was silver bright with cold moonlight which etched trees, brush, and boulders against the ground and the walls of the canyon. The cold waters of the stream rushed swiftly along, murmuring between the grassy banks. The wind swayed the tall trees of the thick bosque that blocked off the right-hand branch of the canyon.

Gallagher picketed the bay, then waded across the stream, hardly feeling the numbing effect of the cold water, with his eyes on that dark bosque. He walked slowly toward it, Sharps at hip level, full-cocked, finger drawing up trigger slack.

He stopped in the thick shadows of the first trees to look and listen. The place was quiet and peaceful, but to him there was a brooding quality about it.

He passed quickly through the wood and reached the far side, stopping while still within the shelter of the trees to look out upon the more open reaches of the branch canyon. Then he caught the faint bittersweet odor of woodsmoke. He looked to his left, up a long gradual sloping of the canyon floor, and his eyes widened as his jaw dropped.

There were several buildings on a broad rock shelf that overlooked the lower portions of the canyon. Smoke drifted lazily up from a chimney at one end of the biggest structure. Water flowed from a large square opening at the floor level of the west building and poured into a rock-walled pool, then overflowed to follow a narrow rock channel down toward the stream at the bottom of the canyon.

The main building was made of great hewn stones, neatly mortared together. There were a few small, secretive windows on the ground-floor level of the two-story house, and between the windows were loopholes. When Gallagher focused the captain's glasses on the scene he saw that the main building was actually two similar structures about fifty or sixty feet apart, connected by a two-story wall which formed a courtyard between the buildings. A great bolt-studded gate was set in the wall closest to Dan.

The place was like a small fort, much like some of the old fortifications in Dan's native Ireland. There were outbuildings, too, placed against a high rock ledge. Corrals were evident beyond this ledge.

High above the main building was a great crescent opening in the live rock of the canyon wall, and he could see a fine example of cliff dwellings placed within the shelter of the huge opening, with dark smoke stains showing clearly against the salmon-colored rock. A threadlike trail which seemed to hang against the side of the canyon wall made its way up to a wide terrace in front of the pile of cliff dwellings.

Gallagher looked away; no one had lived in them for hundreds of years. The other place was different. It looked deserted, but there was that smoke rising from the chimney. Was it possible that the place had been recently abandoned? All of Arizona was in the grip of a cold fear now that the troops had left. The people had either fled to California or to New Mexico. But someone had built a fire in that building.

A cold feeling crept over Gallagher. Stories of haunted canyons and ruins eased insidiously into his teeming mind, and the Celtic superstition of the man began to take hold. It was a curse, and one who is not of that talented yet infinitely superstitious race can ever know what the fertile imagination of such a people can bring to life.

He waited a long time, knowing that the moon soon would be on the wane, leaving him alone in the darkness with that cold-looking mysterious block of buildings. But she might be in there, or whoever lived there might know

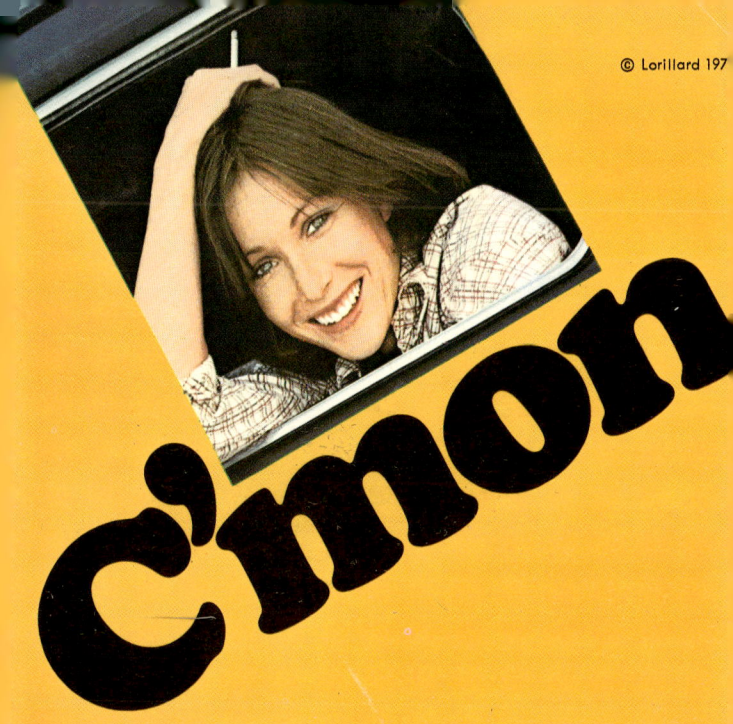

© Lorillard 197

C'mon

Come for the filter. **You'll stay for the taste.**

19 mg. "tar," 1.2 mg. nicotine av. per cigarette, FTC Report Apr. '75.

Warning: The Surgeon General Has Determined That Cigarette Smoking Is Dangerous to Your Health.

Lorillard 1975

I'd heard enough to make me decide one of two things: quit or smoke True.

I smoke True.
The low tar, low nicotine cigarette.
Think about it.

King Regular: 11 mg. "tar", 0.6 mg. nicotine,
King Menthol: 12 mg. "tar", 0.7 mg. nicotine, 100's
Regular: 13 mg. "tar", 0.7 mg. nicotine, 100's Menthol: 13 mg.
"tar", 0.8 mg. nicotine, av. per cigarette, FTC Report April '75.

Warning: The Surgeon General Has Determined That Cigarette Smoking Is Dangerous to Your Health.

where she was. One thing was certain: Apaches would not be in the buildings.

Gallagher stood up and cased the field glasses. He took the carbine and worked his way up the slope within the cover of the woods until he stood about a hundred yards opposite the big gateway. He was now impressed not only with the layout of the place and the excellent manner of its construction but with its great potentialities. A man could live like a feudal baron there. There was everything in plenty—water, fish, grazing, shelter from the heat of summer and the cold winds of winter, timber, and plenty of game.

He eyed the tiny windows and the slitted loopholes. Nothing. Even the mysterious smoke had vanished. The moon now slanted its cold rays down upon the western face of the building next to the wide pond. Gallagher wet his lips. He suddenly looked quickly behind him. The long forgotten lines of "The Ancient Mariner" came drifting silently and quickly into his mind to plague him.

> ". . . walks on,
> And turns no more his head:
> Because he knows a frightful fiend
> Doth close behind him tread."

Gallagher cast the gruesome thought from his mind. "Get on with it, boyo!" he said sharply to himself.

He walked out into the clear moonlight toward the gate. The big man had a set look on his hard Irish face and the glinting of ice in his blue eyes. The crunching of his feet on the hard earth and the sound of his breathing seemed abnormally loud to him, as though he could easily be heard within those walls. *But by whom?*

There was a small doorway cut into the right-hand side of the huge gate. Gallagher stopped and stretched out a hand to try it. It swung open easily at his touch. He hesitated, then quickly stepped inside, swinging head and carbine muzzle from side to side, ready to fire in a split second. There was nothing to fire at. He stood at one end of a deep-walled courtyard between the two massive buildings. Roofed porches ran the entire length of the second floor of each building. Small paned windows looked out upon the porches.

The ground of the courtyard seemed as hard as stone. A huge soap-rendering kettle stood on a stone fireplace. A wagon had been drawn into the yard. The bed had been removed and a number of heavy logs slung to the frame of the running gear. Here and there tools were stored in racks; harness hung from pegs driven into crevices in the stone walls. At the far end, in a corner, a small smithy had been fitted out complete with tools.

Gallagher looked uneasily about him. It was the second time since he had left Fort McComber that he had stumbled onto a place such as this. But there had been dead bodies at Dunlap's place, along with the very live body of the woman Gallagher had grown to love. Here there was nothing but soft furtive echoes.

He looked up over his head. A sentry walk ran from one building to the other just over the gateway, with the top of the wall acting as a solid breastwork. Another such walk ran across the far end of the courtyard. Gallagher nodded in appreciation. Whoever had built this place in remote Canyon Encantado had built a small citadel, ready for a long stay.

He padded forward and stopped in the middle of the courtyard. The place was as quiet as a tomb. He shook his head and walked back toward the little gate. Gallagher poked his head outside and looked about. He wanted no one walking up behind him. He stepped outside and walked a short distance from the wall. It was as deserted out there as it had been when he had reached the buildings.

Gallagher shrugged. He had to go through those buildings, much as he hated the very thought of it. *She* might be in there.

He stepped inside the courtyard and advanced a few feet. The door closed quickly behind him. He whirled. There was no one there. Then he looked up. He saw four bearded men, two on each opposite porch, with rifles in their hands and cold menace in their eyes. They did not speak. For one awful moment Gallagher thought they might be ghosts. Then one of them laughed; laughed right in Gallagher's staring face. Somehing landed hard against his skull, just behind his left ear, and as he felt his carbine fall from his hands and as the ground rushed up at him with incredible swiftness he heard all of them laugh.

Water splashed against Gallagher's face. He opened his eyes to look up into the hard face of a young man. "You weren't hit that hard, bucko," he said with a grin.

Gallagher felt the egg behind his ear and withdrew his hand to look at the blood upon his fingers. "It was me that was hit, not you, boyo," he said sourly.

"Get up. The boss wants to see you."

"Who's the boss?"

"You'll see. Now get up!"

Gallagher got dizzily to his feet. A man stood on the sentry walk over the gateway through which Gallagher had entered. The wind ruffled his beard, and the moonlight glinted from the polished barrel of his rifle.

They had stripped Gallagher of his weapons. He shook his head. He had walked neatly into this mess. Rebels probably, he thought as he walked toward a door indicated by his guard.

The guard opened the door and spoke close to Gallagher's ear. "Don't get any ideas, soldier. We've got enough men to take you apart piece by piece."

"So?"

"*So!*"

"Go . . ." breathed Gallagher.

"Like all the Irish you talk a good fight," said the man as he closed the door behind them.

Gallagher turned slowly, and there was pure cold hell in his eyes. "Maybe ye'd like to try me, boyo?" he asked thinly, and his accent was as thick as porridge.

"Get on with you!" said his guard. "Walk or be driven!"

Gallagher felt a pistol muzzle against one of his kidneys. He walked.

He opened another door at a command from the guard and stepped down into a big room ceiled by huge handhewn beams. A fire had been blazing in the massive fireplace, but now had died to a thick bed of ashes from which a ruby ember eye peered now and then. The room was comfortably warm. A man sat in a chair near the fire with his big veined hands resting on his thighs. His eyes held Gallagher's. There was a cold look about the man despite the warmth of the room. His eyes were cold, his beard was gray, and his thick hair was heavily shot with gray. There was a cold grayness about the man, thought Gallagher, the cold grayness of death. The eyes seemed to clash against Gallagher's as though the man were trying to force his will upon him.

"It was easy, Elijah," said the young man behind Gallagher. "He walked into the trap like a schoolboy." He laughed.

Then Gallagher knew who the man was. It was Elijah Darris, the man who had used the name Dunlap with Ellen. Elijah Darris . . . jackleg preacher, member of some obscure and unsanctified religious sect of strange and outlawed practices, a middle-aged lecher with perverted tastes.

"You know me?" asked Darris.

Gallagher was startled. It was almost as though the man had read his mind. "No," he said quietly.

"You're lying."

"Who . . . me? Ye mistake me."

"I'm Elijah Darris."

"So?"

"You've heard of me?"

"Can't say that I have."

"You're lying again."

Gallagher shrugged. The man seemed a little mad, perhaps insane. From what Gallagher had heard of him it was quite possible that he was mad.

"Who are you?"

"First Sergeant Daniel Gallagher, Provisional Company A, First United States Dragoons, although they call us cavalry now, but I . . ."

"Shut up."

Gallagher reddened and closed his big hands, but the

pistol nuzzled his back like a bloodthirsty kitten snuggled close.

"What are you doing in my country?"

"Yer country?" The pistol muzzle jambed Gallagher's kidneys. He winced. "I'm on me way to California."

"On what business?"

"Why, on me own business! I'm to report to the nearest military post there. Fort Yuma, it would be." Gallagher smiled. "That was the last orders of me commanding officer."

"Where is he?"

"He died."

"And the rest of his command?"

"They will be along soon."

"He's lying again, Elijah," said the man behind Gallagher. "He came into the canyon with the woman, and the Tontos were breathing down their necks. There are no United States troops within hundreds of miles of here. They've all pulled out of Arizona."

Gallagher nodded. They knew as much as he did . . . perhaps more than he did. If they had been watching him all that time they were as good as Apaches, maybe better, for he had never seen them.

"Why did you leave the woman behind?"

Then Gallagher knew they had found her. "I could not take her with me."

"You deserted her?"

"I . . ."

Elijah cut him short with a wave of his left hand.

Gallagher stepped forward. "If ye have the woman ye must turn her over to me for safe conduct to Fort Yuma."

Elijah yawned. "How was Fort Coulter?" he asked.

Gallagher half closed his eyes. He felt like a child in front of this man.

"You might have known there would be no weapons and munitions left there, Sergeant."

"So? Then ye know where they are?"

Darris nodded. "They are safe in my keeping."

"They are the property of the United States. Those supplies must be turned over to me."

"So? Your uniform and stripes do not give you authority over Elijah Darris, Sergeant."

"I can place this area under martial law," bluffed Gallagher.

A cold smile fled across the bearded face. "No . . . you can't. You and your country have no authority here."

"This is part of the United States."

Again the frigid smile. "The United States? They have no authority over a domain they cannot hold. Where are your soldiers, Sergeant Gallagher? Where is your flag?" A thickly veined hand passed back and forth as though brushing away everything he had mentioned. "Gone like an evil stench!"

Gallagher tilted his head to one side. "Ye think so? What are ye then? Mormons?"

"No."

"Rebels?"

"No."

"Then who are ye?"

"I am Elijah Darris!" The fanatic looked at Gallagher as though his short statement would explain everything.

Gallagher wet his lips. The pistol was not against his back, but he could almost feel it. "Ye have the woman here?"

"Yes."

"And her sister Judith?"

There was a queer look in the piercing eyes. "She is here, too."

"Ye took her from the station before Klij-Litzogue struck it?"

"Yes."

"And the other sister?"

There was a strange look on the bearded face. "She would not come peacefully with me."

"Did she die by her own hand or the hand of the Apaches?"

"No, Sergeant."

The answer struck Gallagher like a gun-butt blow. He stared at Elijah Darris, the man who had brutally killed a beautiful young woman because she would not accompany him.

"You understand, Sergeant?"

"Ye filthy woman-chasing lecher!"

Darris stood up. "Get out of here! Your time will come, and the way of your death will not be pleasant. Klij-Litzogue will give much to get his hands on you."

Gallagher froze. He remembered now that Elijah Darris had been known to deal with Klij-Litzogue.

Darris smiled thinly. "It frightens you, doesn't it, Sergeant Gallagher?"

Gallagher did not answer. The man was right. Gallagher felt panic rise in his gorge. He left the room with the guard behind him, who locked him into a small room with a tiny window that looked out upon the pond.

He lay down upon a cot. He was bone-weary. He'd never leave the canyon alive unless it was to be delivered to Klij-Litzogue like a steer for bloody slaughter. But there was a greater sickness underlying even that thought. The idea of Ellen Eustis being a captive in this outpost of hell, a helpless victim of Elijah Darris and his strange lusts, filled him with terror and anguish.

▶▶ *Chapter* 13

THE GREAT house was quiet. It was deepest night, perhaps getting on toward dawn. Gallagher got up off his cot and walked to the door. The wind scrabbled along the eaves and rattled a shutter somewhere. Gallagher reached down for his left shoe and took it off. He bent the sole into an arc and worked the shoe back and forth until the built-in steel brace worked out of the leather. It was good spring steel. He got down on his knees and listened. Not a sound came from the corridor. They would not have left a guard. The walls of the room were thick and strong, and the window was too small.

Gallagher worked silently and patiently, probing into the guts of the door lock with the steel. An hour went past before the end of the piece of steel caught hard on something. He eased the end of it down. There was a dull click. The door opened silently in his grasp.

He stepped into the corridor and took off his other shoe. He tied the shoes together by their laces and hung them about his neck. Gallagher padded to the door which led into the great room where he had first talked to the madman. He padded about looking for a weapon, but there was none to be found.

He crossed the long dining room and tried the next door. It opened into a low-ceilinged kitchen equipped with a great fireplace and several stoves. He armed himself with a heavy-bladed knife, then went back through the rooms to his cell. He rolled the blankets to make it look as though he was asleep, then left the room to work his way down to the end of the corridor.

He eased the door open and looked out into the moonlit courtyard. It was empty of human life, but a fire still glowed in the forge. He was sheltered beneath the second-floor porch. Then he heard the steady thudding of feet on the sentry walk over the north gate, and he knew he'd be spotted as soon as he stepped out into the bright moonlight.

There was another door behind him. He opened it and stepped down into a low-ceilinged room which was damp and smelled like a dairy. He heard the noise of moving water. Moonlight streamed through the loopholes, and he saw that the spring that fed the pond and channel in front of the west building actually started from underneath the house.

He shook his head. They had thought of everything. No Apaches or troops, unless equipped with artillery, could ever take the place by attack or siege. He'd be willing to bet on the deadly marksmanship of those cold-eyed bearded men.

He could see a hint of moonlight on the water at the west end of the stone trough through which the spring flowed to the outside of the house. The water was like the overflow from a glacier, so icy it was. But it was the only way he could get out of his prison.

He took a deep breath, rolled his big body into the trough, and felt his breath leave him as the water closed about his body. He worked his way along the trough until his head stuck out into the moonlight and he saw the flat surface of the pond shining in the light. He pulled himself forward and went head and shoulders down into the pool. It was like bathing in a tub of ice cakes.

He forced himself to swim silently underwater to the far side of the pool, then crawled out on the bank beneath low overhanging trees. He shivered until he could have sworn the sentry could hear his teeth chattering.

The canyon was quiet and still. The wind had died away. Gallagher worked his way through the trees to the south end of the buildings, passed the end of the pond, and flattened himself against the building. The steady tread of a sentry sounded on one of the walks within the courtyard. He bellied along a ledge, then through thick brush until he reached a low line of buildings, where he stopped to look and listen. He had no idea how many men were in the buildings. He was pretty sure how many women were in them, though. Two: Ellen and Judith Eustis.

Gallagher studied the lay of the land. The easternmost house had been built on the hill slope, so the rear of the first floor was below ground and the second floor was at ground level. He could see a doorway at the south end of the second floor. He crawled through the brush. The windows were all heavily shuttered. He could go neither north or south without the likelihood of being seen by guards at either end of the courtyard.

He reached the side the house and looked up at the low eaves. He stood up, gripped the edge, then swung himself up easily to lie flat on the roof. He moved slowly up to the ridge of the roof and peered down into the courtyard from the shelter of one of the large chimneys. He waited until he could see both sentries to make sure they were still at their posts, then slid down the roof, dropped lightly to the ground, and flattened himself against the wall. He edged toward the door, tried it, found it locked.

Gallagher worked his way through the brush to the far end of the low buildings. He walked into the shelter of some trees growing in a low place that led to the stream. He stopped on the bank and suddenly remembered Shannon. He looked up toward the buildings. They could see him if he crossed from his shelter to the big bosque that closed the way to the other branch of the canyon. There was nothing else to do but to swim that frigid stream. He went right in, waded for a moment, then swam with a slow easy breath stroke to the far bank. His teeth were chattering loudly enough to alert everyone in those moonlit buildings on the slope. Gallagher walked quickly into the trees and struck out for the ford where he had left Shannon.

The great bay was gone, as Gallagher had expected. He squatted in the shelter of a boulder. They would know he had escaped when morning came. They'd beat the bloody canyon for him. He knew too much now for them to let him get away. But it was a long time until daylight.

Gallagher set off with long swinging strides. He passed through the bosque and the trees that thickly lined the side of the stream opposite the buildings. Then he reached an area where the stream wound in great loops across flat lands, thickly stippled with brush and scrub trees. He could see the wide mouth of the canyon when he caught the pungent odor of burning mesquite wood. It was certainly an easier way to enter the canyon than the ones he had used.

Gallagher worked his way through the trees like a wraith while the odor of the smoke grew ever stronger. When he saw the huddled figures lying on the ground on the far bank of the stream his blood seemed to congeal. Apaches! A lot of them. Gallagher softly hit the ground and lay on his belly eying the camp. He needed weapons, and they had weapons. There were at least a score of them, however, and few white men could creep up on a camp of these warriors without being discovered.

He was damned if he did and damned if didn't. There wasn't any doubt in his mind that Darris was in close accord with Klij-Litzogue. For Gallagher it was either be caught by Darris to be turned over to Klij-Litzogue, or be caught by the Tonto himself. There was a third alternative. Gallagher could run, strike out for Fort Yuma on his lonesome and to hell with everything.

He rested his tired head on his arms. The mission had not been accomplished. Ellen Eustis had been lost to him and was now in the hands of Darris. To go back was to face such odds that his chances of succeeding were hardly worth thinking about.

The low voice seemed to come from the ground, then from the air, and Gallagher raised his head to listen while the cold sweat burst out upon his body. *"The company has been assigned a dangerous mission . . . most likely a hopeless one . . . but we will obey those orders to the letter . . . if there is one man left, and one only, that man will return the guidon to the regiment . . . but only when the mission has been completed successfully, Sergeant Gallagher!"*

"Yes, sir," he said softly.

There was another voice, that of a woman, the woman he loved. *"Don't you want me?"*

Gallagher's mind reeled. He looked into the sky and caught the first rays of the false dawn. Now there was only one course for him to take. He staggered off into the brush to find a hiding place before the sun came up. He wasn't worried about the Tontos, as long as he kept within the bounds of the forbidden canyon. But Darris and his men would surely be combing the area for him once his escape was discovered.

Chapter 14

IT WAS morning. Gallagher opened his eyes and looked down into the canyon. The stream rushed along far below his position. The ledge he lay upon was hardly wide enough for a man of his build, but he felt safer up there.

He could see the Apache camp. Gallagher shivered at the thought of what Yellow Snake would do to him if he caught him.

But the big, bone-weary, dirty-faced redheaded dragoon was too stupid to quit trying to represent the entire United States Army west of the Rio Grande and east of the Colorado.

A gecko lizard eyed Gallagher brightly as the sun arose. "Are ye fat enough for a meal?" asked Gallagher. The lizard knew when it was in trouble. It vanished into a cleft.

It was then that he saw the horsemen riding down the canyon. There were four of them. White men. The last man of the quartet led a heavily laden pack mule. The eyes of the men constantly scanned the canyon walls and the area beyond the stream. Gallagher knew well enough who they were looking for. He crouched down. His red head would be like a flame in the bright morning sunlight.

They reached the place where the invisible boundary line stretched across the canyon; the taboo line. There they stopped and waited. Some of them lighted pipes and smoked as they waited. The bluish tobacco smoke rose in the windless air.

Klij-Litzogue came through the brush with some of his warriors, and they stopped fifty feet from the waiting white men. During the next half hour one of the white men and the Tonto chief carried on a conversation, principally in sign language. At last the pack mule was brought forward and unloaded, the contents of the packs being laid out on a flat slab of rock. Gallagher whistled softly. Carbines and ammunition boxes, and he was willing to bet he knew well enough the place they had originally come from.

The white men rode back up the canyon as the sunlight began to fill it. The Tontos were examining the fine weapons. Suddenly Yellow Snake raised one and fired it. The report echoed flatly down the canyon, and the slug slapped against a rock not two feet from Gallagher's head. Gallagher winced as tiny shards of lead and rock struck his face. It was a good five minutes before he realized that the Tonto had just fired the carbine at random to try it out, not to plant a slug between Gallagher's bloodshot eyes.

The Tontos carried the weapons and ammunition back to their camp, where the smoke of the cooking fires was now rising straight in the air. They had the canyon corked as far as Gallagher was concerned.

He had other ideas.

When the long day had crept past and the walls of the canyon were thick with shadows he crawled stiffly from his eyrie and headed toward the stream. He lay beside the stream for a long time, alternately sousing his head and drinking deeply of the pure cold water.

The wind was cold when he started up the canyon. He had no fear of the Tontos as long as he stayed within the invisible taboo boundaries, but the men at the buildings were quite another matter. They were potentially as dangerous and a great deal more shrewd. They knew he had little chance of getting past the Tontos. They also knew what he needed no matter what he decided to do. He needed food and weapons first. He needed a horse. He might steal a horse and even some weapons, but in order to accomplish his mission he had to find those weapons. The weapons and the women would be bait enough for Gallagher.

He could see the buildings plainly. There were horses and mules in the corrals. Smoke rose from a chimney.

The dying sun glinted dully on the barrel of a sentry's rifle. Shannon was in the corral, too. There was no mistaking the big bay. There was something else in the corral, lying in the mud and filth in one corner, the once bright colors stained and dull. It was the guidon. "Ye dirty bastards," said Gallagher. He shook a fist at the buildings. "I'll wipe the dung from it on yer faces," he promised.

He crawled through the woods until he could see the foot of the trail which climbed the canyon wall behind the buildings to the cliff dwellings. The place looked peaceful enough, like a country holding in his native Ireland, but to Gallagher there was an aura of obscene evil about it. These men owed no allegiance to their country; they traded weapons to Apaches; they would hold a woman against her will.

It was dark in the canyon when he reached the top of the trail. Yellow light shown from the loopholes and small windows of the buildings far below him. The noise of the stream came to him, and now and then he thought he heard voices, but he was not sure.

The cliff dwellings had been neatly tucked into the great arched opening in the live rock of the canyon wall. It was a far greater ruin than Gallagher had realized. There were several towers, some of them three stories high. Row after row of one-room houses extended the full length of the area, with their tiny windows and distinctive T-shaped doorways. Here and there along the terraced front of the building area he could see the openings that led down into the rounded chambers beneath the ground, with crude ladders protruding from the holes.

The moon had begun to flood the canyon with light. Some of the buildings had collapsed into mounds of adobe and rock from which shattered wooden beams and poles protruded. Most of the other rooms were empty except for smashed pottery, dried bones, and animal droppings.

He entered the ground floor of the tower at the end of the row of dwellings and ascended a thick log that had been notched like a chicken ladder. From the top story he had a fine view of the buildings below, the canyon, and the moonlit stream. There was a second row of buildings behind the first. He descended the ladder and began to look through the rest of the rooms. The moon shown down on the terrace almost as brightly as though it was daylight.

He was at the end of the row, and there was only one big dwelling left to explore. His heart was sick within him. He had been so damned sure the weapons would be stored in the dwellings. He looked into the room. The back wall seemed to be of better construction than any of the other rooms he had been in. The stones were larger, better shaped, and more evenly laid. It wasn't until he was closer to them that he realized his search was over.

They were not stones at all but rather large wooden boxes of a type he knew well. He undid the thumbscrews of the first box and whistled softly when he raised the lid. The bellies of four carbines were there, neatly nested in wooden supports, with the metal covered with grease. They were slant-breeched Sharps carbines, with patch boxes and Maynard tape primers, Caliber .52. "Model 1855," said Gallagher. They looked as though they had never been used.

He looked along the rows of boxes. They were all the same. Beyond the row of carbine boxes were piles of ammunition boxes, several cases of single-shot and revolving pistols, sabers and scabbards, bayonets, boxes of caps, as well as other impedimenta and accessories.

Beyond was another room, the back wall of which was formed by the slanted roof of the cave. Here were racks of Springfield .58 caliber rifles. Gallagher peered through a door on the right. He whistled again, this time louder. Six brass mountain howitzers stood wheel to wheel, with their caissons behind them. Piled against the walls were rammers, buckets, cases of powder charges, rounds of shot, canister and grape, boxes of friction primer tubes, and all the odds and ends necessary to service and fire the stout little pieces.

There was enough armament in the dwellings to arm a flying column, and arm them as well as any United States troops at Fort Yuma—or anywhere else in California short of the forts along the seacoast. With this stolen equipment the rebels had a good chance to accomplish their mission to take the Pacific coast.

Gallagher walked to the terrace and looked down upon the other buildings. What game was Darris up to? He recognized no authority, neither of the United States nor of the Confederacy, and he dealt openly with the Tontos. But the equipment he held belonged to the United States of America, and the United States Army was the only organization that was entitled to use those weapons, *or to destroy them if need be*. The destruction would be undertaken by First Sergeant Daniel Timothy Gallagher, Provisional Company A, First United States Dragoons.

He needed to arm himself before he started his work. So he would draw his weapons from the U. S. property in the dwellings. He walked into the first of the rooms and opened a box of Colt revolving pistols. He was wiping the grease from one of them when he heard the quiet voice behind him.

"Darris is waiting to see you, soldier. Just drop the pistol like a good boy and turn around with your hands in the air." The words were followed by the greasy sounding click-cluck of a gun hammer being cocked close behind Gallagher's back.

Elijah Darris was seated in his big chair, his veined hands resting on his muscular thighs. His cold gray eyes fixed themselves upon Gallagher and sent an eerie crawling sensation along his spine.

"Did you really think you could escape, Sergeant?" asked Darris at last.

"It was worth a try."

"Very clever. But the Apaches drove you back, eh?"

Gallagher could not but help grin at the memory. "I did a little drivin' meself, old whiskers."

A carbine barrel struck him alongside the neck. Gallagher winced with the blow. "Ye scut," he said in a low voice.

Darris leaned back in his chair. "You are getting to be a problem to us," he said quietly.

"You can always let me go."

"We cannot free you, nor can we keep you here."

"Not very popular, am I?"

"The only alternative is death."

"That's what I thought."

"You know too much."

"Aye."

Darris glanced at the fire and studied the leaping flames. "So ye deal with the Apaches," said Gallagher slowly.

"You saw that?"

"Aye."

"Your tongue is your undoing, but then that has always been the way of your people."

" 'Tis true enough," agreed Gallagher wryly. He set his jaw. "Ye've done great harm, Darris. Ye've murdered a young woman who would not yield to ye. Ye've set yerself up here against the United States of America. Ye are keeping two young women here against their wills. Ye keep me a prisoner—a noncommissioned officer of the United States Army on official business. Worst of all, ye not only plan to supply arms and munitions to the ribils, but ye are also giving them to the Tontos. For what purpose, Darris?"

There was a long silence, and the cold gray eyes touched Gallagher's sensitive nerves like the slimy tentacles of some evil creature. "Is there any more to come from that loose mouth of yours, Sergeant?" asked Darris.

"Much more."

Darris looked at Gallagher's guard. "Take this man out into the courtyard. Tell the men to gather there. Yes, and get the women, too! This will be a lesson for all of them."

He was taken out into the moonlit courtyard. The men were there. Two of them stood on the sentry walks. The others leaned against the walls or the posts that held up the second-floor porches. On the porch of the easternmost of the two buildings were two women. One of them he had never seen, but the other he knew well enough. It was Ellen Eustis. The other must be her sister.

"Bart!" called out Darris from the porch of the western building.

A man swaggered forward from the shadows. He was a real broth of a boy, thought Gallagher. "Yes, boss?" asked Bart.

"The lash," said Darris shortly.

It was done quickly. Stripped to the waist, Gallagher was tied to one of the stout posts that supported the porch of the western building. The wind was cold on his flesh as he stood there, the tips of his toes barely touching the ground.

"How many?" asked Bart.

"A dozen, for a start."

Bart took a lash from a hook and ran his thick fingers through the tails of the thing to free them from each other. Then there was a long pause. There was no movement amongst the men or women. It was quiet except for the distant murmuring sound of the stream and the sighing of the night wind about the buildings.

The first stroke hit him when he least expected it. It drove the breath from his body. His back and belly quivered involuntarily as he waited for the next stinging blow. But Bart was a master of his trade. The second, third, and fourth blows came at varying intervals, and each of them struck hard enough to drive what little wind he had left from his body so that his mouth hung open gasping for the thin air.

One of the watching men laughed, then stopped as Gallagher's pain-shot eyes sought his—the pure Irish hell in them was enough to quiet any man.

The blood coursed slowly down his back. "Enough!" cried Ellen Eustis.

Gallagher looked back at her. Her dark hair hung over her shoulders, and her eyes seemed to sparkle in the moonlight.

The next stroke seemed to cut to the very bones. The blood seeped down past the waist band of his trousers and ran slowly down the backs of his legs.

It was timed neatly. The last stroke hit him like a searing tongue of lightning, and at that instant one of the men cut the rope that held him up. He sagged to his knees. Bart walked around in front of Gallagher, passing his fingers through the tails of the lash, freeing them of blood and bits of skin. He started back a little when he saw the look on Gallagher's face. *"Some day, boyo,"* said Gallagher slowly and distinctly, *"I will have the hide and bones av ye for what ye have done to me."*

Bart spat in Gallagher's face, raised a big foot and drove it at Gallagher, catching him on the side of the head and driving him to the blood-spattered ground. He spat again, and there was a low growling sound deep in Gallagher's throat. He came up from the ground like an uncoiling spring. His left fist caught Bart in the belly, and the right came across like a triphammer to meet the downcoming jaw.

Bart swung at Gallagher's face with the lash, but Gallagher twisted it free and began to lay it about the head and shoulders of the man like he was chopping wood. Bart screamed hoarsely.

Three of the men were on Gallagher, but he drove them back with the lash. He brought up a knee into the groin of one of them, smashed the thick handle of the whip down on the head of another, kicked the third man in the belly. Bart rushed in to meet a left to the jaw and a vicious crack alongside the head with the whip handle.

They drove him back at last, fighting savagely in an insensate fury that made him impervious to pain and fatigue. Finally he struck a wall and was driven into a corner. They rushed him, and the overpowering weight of their hard bodies carried him down until he could not move.

"Let me have him!" yelled Bart insanely.

"No!" said Darris. "The water cure will take the heat from him, if it doesn't kill him."

He almost screamed in agony as they dragged him by the legs across the harsh ground to the pond. They hurled him in and stood there grinning as the breath went out of him in a great spluttering gasp.

He sank quickly to the bottom of the icy pool and

then came up to meet hands that thrust him down again and again until he knew he was going to die. And all the time, when he could hear them, they were laughing as though it was some kind of monstrous joke, and the loudest of the laughing ones was the man named Bart.

He was almost gone. He came up for one last fighting try and saw the hard face of Bart close to his. "Had enough, *hombre?*" sneered he.

Gallagher spat full into his face. A fist hit him and drove him under. The water cascaded over the edges of the pond and swept down the slopes as he fought his last fight. He came up for his last sight of the world.

"That's enough!" said a sharp cold voice.

A man stood at the south end of the pond with a long-barreled rifle held at waist level. His wide-brimmed hat shielded his face.

"Who the hell are you?" demanded Bart.

"Luke Ainsley."

"We been expecting some of you boys."

"What are you doing to him?"

"Punishing him," said Bart with a grin.

"Pull him out."

Gallagher lay quietly getting back his breath. "Hello, Luke," he said at last.

"Good God! It's Gallagher himself!"

"The same," said Gallagher wearily.

"They said you were dead."

"Who did?"

"Them back at Fort McComber."

Gallagher looked quickly at the man. "They tried hard enough to kill me. Lucky you came. Matthew, Mark, *Luke,* and John, they guard the bed I lie upon."

"Very funny," said Bart. He looked at Ainsley. "Darris ain't going to like you butting in like this, Ainsley."

The man spat. "I'm worried," he said quietly.

They eyed the lean man and his steady rifle. They shuffled their feet.

"Take him to one of them buildings over there," said Ainsley, jerking his head toward the row of low structures.

"Darris won't like this."

The rifle hammer clicked back. "Move!" snapped Ainsley.

They carried him to the end building and dumped him on a dusty cot. As they left he was sure he could hear the thin screaming of a woman from somewhere in the bigger buildings. He tried to get up, but Ainsley came in and shook his head. "Stay put, Gallagher," he said. "Even *you* can't fool around with these bearded bastards."

Gallagher cursed and lay flat. The raw meat of his back was seared by the rough blanket on the cot. He was sick and exhausted, but that scream struck through his mind worse than the pain of his big body.

▶▶ Chapter 15

AINSLEY squatted beside the door and lighted a candle. "They've been looking for you, Gallagher."

"Who?"

"Them at Fort McComber."

"They couldn't look for me, Luke. No horses. Hardly enough men to penetrate Tonto country anyways."

Luke shielded the guttering flame. "You mean *your* company?"

"Aye."

"That's not who I meant."

Gallagher winced as his body warmed up a little.

"Roll over," said Ainsley. He felt in a pouch at his waist and brought out a small pot. He came to the cot and began gently to rub ointment on the raw back. "Jesus God," he said. When he was done he bandaged the back and covered Gallagher with a blanket.

Gallagher wiped the cold sweat from his face. "Listen, Luke," he said quickly. "These men have the missing stores from Fort Coulter. They are trading guns to the Tontos, and I think they will sell or trade the rest of the weapons and stores they have to the ribils. Now look ye! Ye are like a ghost in the deserts and the mountains. Go ye to Fort Yuma and get troops to come back here and destroy these weapons!"

"You're talking loco, Gallagher."

Gallagher stared at the man, and his mind began to clear. How would Ainsley know about the missing weapons from Fort Coulter? He had been a civilian scout for the Army before the war, but he had not been around for some time.

Ainsley squatted on his heels again. "Just what is this you want me to do?"

"There are weapons stored here, Luke. Weapons that can turn the Tontos into a scourge that will sweep all of Arizona, or weapons that will help the rebels conquer Arizona and the Pacific Coast! Get to Fort Yuma and get troops!"

"Why should I go?"

Gallagher stared at him. "Ye can see I can't go! Besides, they mean to kill me."

"So?"

"Ye are an Army scout, Luke. It's up to ye!"

"I'm a scout all right, Gallagher, but not for the United States Army. I am scouting for Captain Hunter Sherrod, commander of G Company, Sixth Texas Mounted Rifles, Army of the Southwest."

"What 'J' Company outfit is that?" Then a cold light dawned in Gallagher's mind.

Ainsley smiled. "You have quite a distinction, Gallagher, as Lieutenant Artenis said, a little sarcastically of course. There are no United States troops left in Arizona except *you*, Gallagher, and the prisoners at Fort McComber, and most of them are dying of typhoid."

"Artenis?"

Ainsley nodded. "What the hell did you do to him, Gallagher?"

The big hands closed and opened, closed and opened. "Nothing to what I'd like to do," said Gallagher softly. He looked at Ainsley. "And they sent you ahead to this place to find the weapons."

"They were never lost, mick."

"Aye."

"All's fair in love and war, Gallagher."

"Aye. But the Tontos? They hold the mouth of the canyon. They will not come in here. But they will not let the ribils pass into here either, will they?"

"Darris has arranged that."

"I might have known," breathed Gallagher. He closed his eyes.

"We can use good men, Gallagher. You know this country better than I do. I would have thought Lieutenant Artenis might have persuaded you to join us. I was surprised when he sent for me. You're on a losing side, mick. Reconsider."

"What do ye offer me?"

"They said they had a commission for you. What do you say, Gallagher? Captain Sherrod authorized me to tell you that, if I found you."

The blue eyes opened and held Ainsley with a terrible gaze. "I came here from Ireland, a starving kid, without a seat to me breeches or a shilling in me pockets. They tuk me into the Army and made a man out of me. I earned me three stripes and diamond the hard way. I've worn the blue and served under the blessed Stars and Stripes too long to change now."

"You're a fool! If I leave you here with Darris and his men they'll kill you or turn you over to Klij-Litzogue. You know how badly *he* wants you."

"Aye." Gallagher sat up and gripped the edge of the cot. "Let them kill me, or torture me, but they will do it when I am wearing *blue,* Ainsley! Now get out of here before I break yer goddam traitorous neck between me hands like a matchstick!"

Ainsley shrugged. He closed the door behind him and shot the outer bolt.

Gallagher bent his head and held his battered face in his hands. There was more connivery going on than he had realized. Now he had rebels, Tontos, and Darris and his men to contend with. One man, *one* United States dragoon, was still left with enough life within him to fight on.

The thought of Ellen Eustis came swiftly to him. Maybe it had been her who had screamed so desperately. Maybe Darris was already pawing her soft white body. Gallagher's big hands opened and closed spasmodically, and the power in them was terrible to see.

His back had stiffened, and it was an agony to get up and peer from a window. He could see a sentry pacing the length of the southern walkway. The moon was waning swiftly. He looked up the trail that led to the cliff dwellings and the invaluable cache of arms that might mean the difference between victory and defeat for the Union in

California if the rebels got them. There was no hate in Gallagher for Luke Ainsley and Sherrod Hunter, for they were sworn rebels doing their duty as they saw it. It was the others like Millard Artenis and Elijah Darris whom he hated with all the venom in his soul.

He gripped the bars of the window. They were solid. They were solid all right, *but they were made of wood*.

He knew well enough he could not cut through that dense, close-grained wood with the spring steel from his other shoe, but Gallagher set to work anyway.

It was pitch dark when he heard the soft footfall. He stopped cutting and flattened himself against the wall.

"Tsst! Tsst! Tsst!" came the sibilant Apache scout warning.

Gallagher wet his dry lips.

"Tsst! Tsst! Tsst!"

Something brushed against the outside of the wall. *"Mick?"* came the soft question.

"Ainsley?"

"Yes. Come close to the window."

He could just make out Ainsley's head and shoulders against the darkness.

"They are changing the guard," said the scout.

"So?"

"They mean to do away with you."

"That's not surprising."

There was a pause. "I can't stand by and let them do it, mick."

"Gracias, Luke."

"Take this."

Gallagher touched the cold steel of a heavy bowie knife.

"I'm heading back to Captain Sherrod's camp out beyond the canyon. We'll be coming back tomorrow for the weapons. I overheard Darris tell Bart to do away with you."

"So?"

Another pause. "Bart means to turn you over to Klij-Litzogue."

"Jesus God!"

"Now listen to me: Cut your way out of there. Go north up the canyon. Somewhere up there is a hidden trail that will take you out of this accursed canyon. Get out of here and head west to Fort Yuma."

"What about the women?"

Ainsley shifted a little. "Forget about them."

"I can't do that, Luke!"

Ainsley looked back over his shoulder. "Look," he said harshly. "I've given you a chance to live. Get out of here. Go back to the Army. Forget the women. You hear me, mick?"

"Aye."

"I sure wish you'd join up with us, Gallagher."

"Not a chance."

"*Adios*, then."

"*Adios*."

The scout was gone like a ghost.

Blood was running down Gallagher's fingers when he cut through the last of the hard wooden bars. It was black as the pit outside. The wind had died away.

He eased his big shoulders through the window and felt with his raw hands for the ground. He worked his slim hips through the opening and lay flat upon the ground. The main buildings showed as a dark mass against the cliff. He bellied slowly away, gripping the knife. A nocturnal animal scuttled for cover. An owl flitted silently overhead. Somewhere far up on the canyon a coyote howled.

He wormed his way up the slopes until he lay in a hollow not far from the easternmost of the two buildings. It took all of his guts to force himself to work toward the house. If Bart caught him and turned him over to Klij-Litzogue . . . he remembered too well some of the bloody human wreckage he had seen after Apache torture sessions—Old Man Willis, who had been cooked alive over his own stove at Vaca Creek; Corporal Harris of Company A, who had been captured in the lonely Grindstones and staked naked on a hill of big vicious Sonoran ants, with a trail of honey leading to his mouth that had been propped open by a stick sharpened at both ends. As an added touch they had sliced off his eyelids so that the intense sunlight would burn away his sight while he still lived.

He slid down the slope, driving all such thoughts from his mind. If he kept on thinking about them he'd run like a craven for the shelter of the northern canyon and the hidden trail.

He reached the small door. It was still locked. He swung himself up onto the shingled roof and lay flat. He didn't know what to do now. Then a questing hand struck a raised portion of the roof. He investigated it by feel. "By the powers," he said softly, "a trapdoor, and the bloody thing is not fastened!"

He lifted it gently, and the warm air flowed up about him. He slid it back and peered into the darkness. He was almost sure he could smell the soft aura of feminine flesh. He listened and heard nothing.

Gallagher chewed at his lower lip. He hated the thought of going down into that pit of darkness, but he had to go if he wanted to find those women. Gallagher lay flat, listening and peering down into the rectangle of darkness. It was as quiet as a graveyard, and the simile sent a cold shiver across Gallagher's lacerated back. It was too damned quiet to suit him. Maybe they had set a trap for him down there. But then they didn't know he had escaped again . . . or did they?

The big Irishman gripped the edges of the trapdoor and let himself down easily. His legs swung back and forth feeling for obstacles and a landing place. He breathed a short prayer and let himself drop to the unseen floor. As he rose to get his balance he felt arms wrap themselves about his body from the rear and felt a soft body press tightly against him. Gallagher reacted like an uncoiling spring, turning and gripping for the throat, and his hands brushed naked breasts and long hair.

"Please get me out of here," she said.

Gallagher's heart slammed back and forth within his rib cage like a frightened bird. "Ellen!" he gasped.

"No. It's Judy. Judy Eustis, Ellen's sister."

He gently loosened her arms from about his waist. She was naked he well knew. "Have ye no clothing, lass?" he asked hoarsely.

"No. They stripped me and kept me locked up. I managed to get free and find my way up here. I couldn't find any clothing."

He stared at the vague dimness of her face. "What have they done to ye?"

She looked away. "It was *him*," she said quietly.

"Darris?"

"Yes."

He nodded. Darris had a reputation for such things. Maybe Ellen was next. "Where are we?" he whispered. "Tell me the layout av this house."

"This is an attic. We are almost in the middle of it. There is a door in the wall behind you that leads to a large storeroom. At the far end of the storeroom there is a ladder leading down to the second floor."

"Where is Ellen?"

"I'm not sure."

"Think!"

She seemed to stiffen in the darkness. "Why should I? If it hadn't been for her this would never have happened."

"I don't understand. She was much concerned about ye."

"Oh certainly! Ellen always has been concerned about me! That's why she hauled Evelyn and me out to this hell on earth! Evelyn is just as bad. She doesn't care what happens to me."

"Evelyn is dead, lass."

"She's well out of this mess then! I've heard these men talk about you, Sergeant. They're afraid of you. They say if you escape you'll have the Army down on their heads."

"Aye."

"Will you take me away from here?"

"I'll try."

She came closer to him. "Then let's go! Right now!"

"I must find your sister."

"If you look for her they'll catch you."

He placed his hands on her smooth bare shoulders. "It is a risk I must take, Judith."

She sobbed softly, and he drew her close to comfort her. Her arms crept about his neck, and he felt her breasts and belly press against him as though she was a bordello girl from Tucson. "Forget about Ellen," she said softly. "Just get *me* out of here. You won't be sorry, Sergeant. Help me get up through that trapdoor. They say you know this country as well as any Apaches do. I can hide out in the canyon until you get horses. The Apaches won't come in here. Surely you can find some way to get me back to civilization if anyone can."

A slow flame crept up his belly and back. He pushed her back a little. "Ye're daft, lass."

"Am I? Are you a big enough fool to try and find her in this hellhole?"

"Aye, that I am," he said simply. "I brought Ellen into this mess, and by the powers, I intend to get her out of it! As for ye, shameless little baggage that ye are, I'll take ye along, too, gentleman that I am." He walked about the little room. "Are there no clothes here at all?"

She laughed. "Nervous? There's a blanket over there."

He tossed it at her.

She laughed again. "You want me to wrap myself in this filthy thing?"

" 'Tis better than being mother naked in front av a man, is it not?"

"Oh Sergeant! I really don't know!"

He slapped her across the face. "Ye little slut! Wrap yerself in that blanket!"

She moved quickly. Her fingernails raked his face, and he felt the blood run. He gripped her by an arm, twisted it, turned up her bare bottom, and with one calloused hand struck true and flat on the soft rounded flesh and with the other hand gripped across her mouth. He winced as her teeth dug into the hand.

Gallagher released her and walked to the door. He eased it open and walked across the next room, bowie knife in hand. The ladder was there, as she had said it was. A trapdoor had been neatly fitted about the opening in the floor. He lay down and pressed his ear to one of the cracks. There was nothing to hear.

She was close behind him as he stood up. "What is below?" he asked.

"A large room. Some of the men sleep there."

"Are any of them down there now?"

"I'm not sure, but I don't think so."

He pulled up the trapdoor and eased himself down the ladder. Embers glowed in a fireplace, but there was no sign of man in the place. Several bunks had been built against a wall. He crossed to a door leading to the next room and held his ear against it. Nothing. He eased it open and walked into another big room, empty except for a few boxes and some bundles of rags.

It was the same in the next room. A stairway led downstairs from one corner. He went softly down the stairs and found himself in a small room wherein a candle lantern flickered on a table.

The building seemed deserted. He gently opened a door to the courtyard.

He heard the shuffling of the sentry's feet. Judith pointed upward and opened her mouth to scream. He looked away, then crossed the yard like a great lean cat, close to the wall, with the girl just behind him. They stopped beneath the porch of the western building. They had not been seen.

He wanted to get away from this place and away from Judy Eustis, but Ellen was still a prisoner and in the hands of Darris, and if what Gallagher suspected was true there was no time for him to waste.

Chapter 16

GALLAGHER entered the room where the spring water flowed through the stone trough. The girl shivered in the dampness. "Are ye glad now ye put on that blanket?" he asked with a malicious grin.

"Are you?" she boldly asked.

He walked to the next door. She was hardly more than a girl, yet her actions could be those of a much older woman, one with a helluva lot more experience. Then he remembered the words of Ellen Eustis when she had spoken about her youngest sister. *"I think she is still alive. Judy has a way of doing things just like that. Judy likes men."*

Judy Eustis was a bit of a wanton, he knew now. She thought only of herself. She had a way of working a man. He remembered how she had pressed her young body against his and the shameless words she had used. She could make a man forget quite a bit—his duty, his honor, and his soul. God help the man who took her for his wife.

The entire first floor of the western building was empty of life. There was a big kitchen in the southern end with a stairway leading up to the second floor. Gallagher softly ascended it. Judy was not behind him. There was no time to look for her. He reached the top of the stairs and found a sort of sitting room. There was a door on the far wall, and as he walked toward it he heard the distinct sound of flesh striking flesh. Something clattered on the floor. He heard the sound of heavy breathing.

"Get back, you devil!" said a woman. It was Ellen Eustis.

Gallagher hit the door with a shoulder and hurtled into the room. Ellen Eustis stood against a far wall, her dress hanging in rags about her waist and her arms covering her bare breasts. Her face was scratched and bruised. Sweat dewed her flesh. She held a heavy wrought-iron candlestick in one hand.

Elijah Darris stood facing Ellen, reaching out for her with big veinous hands. He whirled in time to meet a smashing right to the whiskers that drove him back against the wall. Gallagher grunted deep in his throat and hit the older man again. Elijah Darris went down on one knee, snatched up a heavy stool, and threw it with all his strength at Gallagher. It bounced off Gallagher's head, almost stunning him, and then the older man closed in, kicking, striking, and cursing.

The old bastard was strong, with muscles like steel wires. He drove Gallagher back toward a great bed and pushed him heavily on top of it. The musty sour smell of the bedding sickened him. He rolled away and planted a foot in the older man's lean belly just as the stool smashed down on the place where Dan's head had been an instant before.

The air went out of Darris with a rush. He hit the wall and bounced back right into a rocky fist that smashed lips and nose together in a bloody froth. He opened his mouth to yell and shut it again as a left sank into his lean belly. Then Gallagher remembered how Darris had stood on the porch like a god and watched his back being lashed into tatters. A right seemed to whistle as it hit the older man. Darris' legs flew up from under him, and he hit hard on the floor with his mouth gaping and blood smeared on his yellow teeth.

She was in Gallagher's arms, forgetting her half nakedness. "Oh, Gallagher," she sobbed. "That man. The awful things he said. He's mad!"

"I've found Judy. We've got to get out of here!"

He led her down the stairs and through the kitchen and the other rooms. Judy was gone. He looked back at Ellen. "Judy is quite a lass," he said.

She nodded. "I can tell you know her, Gallagher."

"She is not like ye, Ellen."

"She is not my real sister. My father brought her home when she was just a little girl," she said quietly. She looked away. "We never really knew whether she was his natural child or. . . . My mother accepted her. She was like that. She never spoke about it, but it broke her heart. Judy has always been trouble for us."

He drew her close. "Ye must know the chances of us getting out of here are almost nil. I can get ye and yer sister out of these buildings, but it will not be long before they scour the canyon for us. They will not harm ye and Judy, but as for me. . ."

Her eyes were fierce in the dimness. "Harm us? If they do catch us, Gallagher, I hope they kill us! That old man is evil itself!"

He grinned. "Spoken like a thoroughbred!"

They stopped in the damp spring room, and Gallagher padded to the door and looked out. The courtyard was deserted, but he could have sworn he saw something move just inside a door across it. Judy. He turned to Ellen. "Ye must follow me close, directly beneath the sentry walk. If I stop ye must stop. If they jump me ye must make a break for it, lass. There are ribil troops coming into the canyon tomorrow. Try to get to them, *but do not go too far.* The Tontos are at the canyon mouth. They will not come in, but do not stray into their camp."

"I won't leave you, Gallagher!" she whispered fiercely.

He kissed her. He stepped outside, flattened himself against the wall, and looked toward the southern sentry walk. It was empty. They crossed the courtyard and entered the small armory room. Still no sign of Judith.

They walked quietly up the stairs. Judith stood in the room, waiting for them. Her face was set. "What do you expect to do now?" she coldly asked Gallagher.

"Get the both of ye out of here."

"*Two* of us? It will be almost impossible to get *one* of us out of here, and you know it!"

"I know who I'd like to leave behint," he said under his breath. "What do ye expect me to do? Sprout wings and fly out av here?"

"Take *one* of us," she said in an odd voice.

He thrust his face close to hers. "Listen to me! I'm

taking the two av ye from here. I will do the best I can. But both of ye will go!"

She smiled coldly. "Choose between us, Sergeant."

"Ye're mad!"

"You must choose!"

He looked back at Ellen. "What is wrong with her?"

"I don't know. She acts strangely at times."

"I do?" spat out Judy.

Gallagher placed a hand across her pretty mouth. "Come," he said to Ellen. He released his grip on Judy. "Will ye be quiet now?"

"You won't choose then?"

"If I did," he said slowly and with emphasis, "it would not be *ye*."

Her face became a terrible, almost degrading thing to see, and then she emitted a piercing scream that could have aroused the dead.

"Mother av God!" said Gallagher hoarsely. He gripped Ellen by the arm and drove a door aside with his shoulder. Judith was still screaming like a soul demented.

"Wait for her!" said Ellen.

"Are ye mad, too?"

He reached the door that led out onto the side of the slopes and fumbled with the bar across it. He jerked the door open and jumped through the opening, hauling Ellen behind him.

The rifle muzzle struck his chest right at the sternum and held him poised on one foot like a ballet dancer in a tableau. "Stay right where you are," said the man who held the rifle.

"I wasn't thinking of going anywhere," said Gallagher as the cold sweat broke out on his body.

"Back into the building!"

Gallagher and Ellen were marched through the building and into the courtyard. Elijah Darris stood there fully dressed with pure icy hell on his bearded face. "I should have let them kill you," he said.

"Kill me then, ye lecherous old bastard!"

There were four more of the men in the courtyard now.

There was death in their eyes. Gallagher's string had run out for sure this time.

Darris raised a hand. "You've broken too many of our laws to live, Sergeant," he said quietly.

"Get on with it, ye old blackguard! Don't prate to me of yer laws. Yer day will come, and though I be dead, me ghost will come back to watch that day."

"I make the decisions and laws here."

Mad as a hatter, thought Gallagher. He was a man trying to build a world of his own because he could not live in the world of other people.

"I sentence you to life imprisonment."

Bart stepped forward. "Kill him and be done with it," he said. "Or still better, turn him over to Yellow Snake."

"When I said 'life imprisonment' I did not say how *long* that life was to be."

They were all watching Darris now. There was something evil about the older man. He smiled, but there was no mirth in his eyes. "There are many small rooms up on the cliffs," he said at last. "Some of them are fitted only with doors. Some of them are placed far back into the rock."

An aura of stinking evil seemed to hover about Darris, somewhat like the foul stench of his big bed. "Throw him into a cell," he said. "In the morning we will wall up this great hulk of a man in a room so small he will hardly be able to move. We will leave a breathing hole and perhaps a hole big enough to admit enough water and hard bread to keep him alive long enough to repent his sins. But he will go mad long before he dies."

They drove Gallagher into a cell and slammed the door behind him. He dropped onto the bare cot and lay for a long time with his hands locked behind his head, staring at the ceiling, waiting to hear the first scream from a woman.

They came for him in the morning and hustled him out of the building and up the trail. The canyon was beautiful under the bright light of morning. The trees waved gracefully in the wind. The stream rippled and flashed under the sunlight. Everything was sharp and cameo clear. It was a hell of a day for a man to know his future as Gallagher did.

The place they had picked for his prison was seemingly wedged into a great crevice. A small T-shaped door led into a room hardly large enough for a man of Gallagher's size to fit into, much less move around in. They dragged him into it and cut his bonds.

"Wall him in!" snapped Darris.

They worked quickly and well, fitting in the lower stones and mortaring them thickly. Higher and higher went the courses until there was but one stone left to be slipped into place. It didn't seem real, this mad business, and yet it was happening.

The wind shifted, and Gallagher could have sworn he heard faint voices in the distance.

"It's Hunter Sherrod and his boys," said one of the men.

Gallagher's heart leaped.

"They're early," said Bart.

"Tell them we are busy," said Darris.

"Too late. Sherrod and Ainsley are coming up the trail."

"Finish the job!" snapped Darris. There was a pause. "Leave no opening."

"Ah, God!" said Gallagher hoarsely.

"What are you doing there, Darris?" asked a soft Texas voice.

"It doesn't concern you, sir," said Darris.

"Likely they're hiding some of the weapons," said Ainsley. "They've been trading some of them off to the Tontos."

"Don't place that last stone," said the officer.

"This is my land," said Darris, "and my business. Let be!"

There was a moment's silence. "What exactly do you mean by that, Mister Darris, suh?" asked the officer.

"This is my country. My domain. I make the laws. I rule. You have no right to tell me what to do, Captain."

The officer's voice was level. "Ainsley told me something about this situation. This territory is now part of the

Confederate States Territory of New Mexico, by conquest. As such, the laws of the Confederate States of America apply here, and as the chief representative of those states here in Arizona I warn you that any claims you make that this is your land and your country are entirely contrary to the laws of the Confederacy."

Gallagher managed a croaking sound from his dry throat.

"What was that?" asked Captain Sherrod.

"Place the stone!" said Darris.

Something clicked—a gun hammer being cocked. "Let me just take a look in there," said Sherrod. "I have twenty-five men down in the canyon, Darris."

Gallagher croaked again. He saw the opening get blocked and for one awful instant thought it was the last stone. "Christ!" he screamed.

"Jesus God!" said Sherrod. "There's a man in there!"

"I have a damned good idea who it is, too," said Ainsley.

"Rip out those stones," said the Confederate officer.

"No!" screamed Darris. "This is my country! I make the laws. I punish transgressors! I am the ruler here! Seize these two men!"

Ainsley spoke in a low voice. "The first man who moves will trigger a bullet into this loco old bastard's back. *Now move those stones out of there!*"

The stones were torn out one by one, and Captain Sherrod reached in, gripped Gallagher beneath the armpits, and dragged him outside into the bright blessed sunshine. The officer unhooked a canteen from his belt and held it to Gallagher's cracked lips.

"For God's sake, Gallagher," said Luke, "I've seen you in some bad situations, but nothing like this!"

Gallagher grinned crookedly. "I have a way of doing these things it seems."

The officer and the scout helped Gallagher down the twisted trail. Sherrod's Company G lounged about on the ground beside the big houses. They wore slouch hats and badly fitting dusty gray uniforms, but they were all fine looking men, young and vital.

"G Company, Sixth Texas Mounted Rifles, Army of the Southwest," said the officer with a note of pride in his voice.

Gallagher, as a professional, noted their weapons, and he knew now why they needed the hidden arms so desperately. Some of them were armed with double-barreled shotguns, some with muzzle-loading Enfield or Springfield musketoons. A few of them had revolving pistols, but most of them carried one or two muzzle-loading single-shot pistols converted from flintlock to percussion lock. Klij-Litzogue and his Tontos were better armed by far than this outfit.

There was another officer standing near the pond, holding the bridle reins of a fine gray horse, and his hard eyes studied Gallagher. It was Millard Artenis wearing Confederate gray. The warmth of the sun and of his miraculous release from the tomb suddenly left Gallagher under the cold thrust of those eyes. Faint bruises still showed on the handsome face of the officer, bruises placed there by the smashing fists of Dan Gallagher. He knew Artenis's warped sense of honor would have to be satisfied, wiped out in the blood of the man who had beaten him and humiliated him.

"Sergeant Gallagher," said Artenis mildly. "We meet again."

"Aye."

"I did not think you could survive, but somehow you did."

"The luck av the Irish, sir." The "sir" had slipped out.

"Maybe your luck has run out at last. The last man of Company A."

"So?"

"The rest are dead, dying, or are prisoners."

"Aye."

Artenis placed a hand on the holster flap of his sidearm. "So stand to your glasses steady," he said softly. "Here's a health to the living. Hurrah for the next man to die."

Elijah Darris and his men had come down the hill and entered the courtyard of the twin houses. The thick gates had closed behind them, and the bars falling heavily across their supports. Now Darris appeared on the sentry walk and looked down at the Texans.

Captain Sherrod looked up. "I'll get those weapons and be on my way, Darris. I'll sign a form authorizing you payment for the storage of the weapons and accessories. My government will reimburse you. I want to get out of this canyon as quickly as possible. I don't want to make camp for the night until I've put a lot of miles between me and those Tontos."

Darris did not speak.

The officer slapped his gauntlets against his thigh. "I'll need water and rations. We'll pay for the rations."

There wasn't a sound or a movement from Darris.

"Do you hear me, suh?"

Darris said nothing but pointed up toward the cliff dwellings. The sun glinted on gun barrels thrust over the terrace wall, and the wind moved the beards of the men who were behind those rifles watching the Texans.

Sherrod looked up at Darris. "What does this mean, suh?"

Gun barrels protruded from the loopholes of the buildings. The troopers slowly got to their feet and backed away from the menacing muzzles.

Darris rested his forearms on the wall. "I have told you that this is my country . . . that I make the laws. Those guns in storage are mine, to do with as I see fit."

Sherrod had been neatly foxed. A hundred men could not have taken those massive twin buildings by assault.

"I can go back south," said the officer easily, "and bring up more men and artillery."

There was a cold, knowing smile upon the bearded face. "Do," said Darris politely, "but it is only fair to warn you that Klij-Litzogue and his Tontos block the canyon mouth, and he will continue to do so until I send word that you may pass."

Ainsley whistled softly. He looked at Gallagher. "He has us by the short hairs, mick."

"Aye," said Gallagher dryly.

"What is it you want from us, Darris?" asked Sherrod.

"You and your men may camp beside the stream, but

no closer than two hundred yards from this western house. I will sell you food."

"Agreed."

Darris clasped his veinous hands together. "In return, I want an assurance from you that my men and I will not be bothered by you or your men, nor forced to obey the laws of the Confederacy."

"You will not be bothered by our forces if you turn over the weapons that rightfully belong to us. I cannot assure you, suh, that you will not have to obey our laws."

Darris straightened and pointed toward the stream. "Go and make your camp. I'll give you until moonrise to agree to my terms."

"What do you intend to do with those weapons?"

Darris smiled crookedly. "Everybody seems to want them. The United States, the Confederacy, the Tontos, and Mister Artenis."

"Mister Artenis is an officer in my command. It was he who made the deal with you to bring those weapons here in good faith, Darris."

"Oh *did* he?"

Hunter Sherrod turned slowly and looked at Millard Artenis, and there was a cold set look on his face. "Well, suh?"

Artenis waved a hand. "I expect something for my services, Captain."

"What, for example?"

"A higher rank in the Confederate Army, for one thing. Payment for these weapons ... in gold."

The Texan's face whitened beneath his tan. "I understood that you, suh, were a patriot."

Artenis smiled. "Oh, I am! I am indeed! But I'm also a poor man, Captain. Gambling and drinking, you know. The Confederacy needs those weapons. I can make a deal with Darris so that you can have them."

In the silence that followed Hunter Sherrod dropped his hand to the butt of his pistol. "Sergeant Gerry," he said quietly.

"Yes, suh!"

"Arrest that man!"

Gerry turned, but Elijah Darris leaned over the wall. "If anything happens to Mister Artenis there will be no deals of any kind. There will be no food for your men. Klij-Litzogue will be told to hold your command back, Captain Sherrod."

Sherrod's hand dropped. He nodded shortly.

Artenis walked slowly toward the small gate set in one of the big gates.

"Damned traitor!" said a red-faced corporal.

"Twice," said Gallagher softly. "Twice."

"One other thing, Captain," said Darris clearly. "By moonrise you must turn over to me the person of Sergeant Gallagher to do with as I see fit."

"Move out!" snapped the officer. He looked up at Darris, slapped gauntlets against thigh, and then followed his command. Gallagher followed the officer, noting that a trooper fell in close behind, his carbine held casually pointing at Gallagher's back.

There were black looks on the dusty faces of the young Texans as they made their camp. Now and then they looked at those strong buildings bright in the sunlight. It had been a long journey from Mesilla to Arizona, and a more dangerous one to Canyon Encantado, and now they had failed in their mission, as Gallagher had failed in his.

Chapter 17

DARKNESS was settling into the great trough of the canyon. The Texans lay about their fires, frying their bacon in iron spiders, brewing strong issue coffee, the while eying the cold stone walls.

Gallagher ate with Captain Sherrod and Luke Ainsley. "The moon will be up before long," said Sherrod softly. "Maybe we can rush them with volunteers."

"Not a chance," said Gallagher. "The place is like a citadel."

Sherrod eyed Gallagher. "You think he'd really turn those Apaches against us?"

"Without a doubt, Captain."

"They were watching us all the time we rode into the canyon," said Ainsley.

"I didn't see any of them," said Sherrod.

"They were there, Captain."

"Who is this Darris anyway, suh?" asked Sergeant Gerry as he stopped beside the fire.

Sherrod looked at Ainsley.

Ainsley was filling his pipe. He placed it between his teeth and lighted it. "He's wanted in half a dozen states for white slavery, larceny, forgery, and murder, too, as far as I know."

"He's a murderer, all right," said Gallagher. He had his memory of Evelyn Eustis.

"Darris found out that the Mormons who had built this place wanted to move on. He bought it from them, lock, stock, and barrel."

"And Artenis made a deal with Darris to store the weapons here," said Sherrod. "Neat as mutton."

The sergeant nodded. He looked up at the buildings. "And where does it place us, suh?" he quietly asked.

It seemed to all of them that the wind had suddenly become quite chilly.

"I must have those weapons!" said Sherrod. He smashed fist into palm.

Gallagher emptied his coffee cup. "Seems as though ye will need all the luck ye can get to escape from this canyon alive, sir, much less try to get those weapons."

They were miles and miles from safety. There were few enough Confederate troops in Arizona. In fact, from what Gallagher had heard Sherrod's Company G was about the only rebel force in the territory.

"I can lie to him," said the officer thoughtfully . . . "give him a written assurance that he will not be bothered by our government."

"Aye," said Gallagher. " 'Twould be fair enough in war."

"He wants you, too, as part of his deal, Gallagher."

"Aye."

"You know what that means."

"I do."

"Take the oath of allegiance to the Confederacy and it will place you squarely under the protection of my government."

"And if I don't?"

They all looked at him.

Gallagher shook his head. "Ye would not turn me over to him. Ye may be ribils, but ye are men."

The officer nodded. "I won't do it," he said. He eyed the big redheaded noncom. "But reconsider, Gallagher. I need officers. If I get those weapons I'll get all the recruits I need. I will be advanced in rank and probably be given a semi-independent command here in Arizona. I can't think of a better man, from what I have heard, to be an officer in my command, Gallagher. Give me your hand on it!"

Gallagher stood up. "That I cannot do, sir. I am a soldier of the United States Army and I will not break my oath of allegiance to my country."

Sherrod dropped his hand. "I didn't think you would break it."

"However," said Gallagher thoughtfully, "there are two

women in that hellhole up there that I must save. I cannot do it alone. I will form an alliance with ye, sir. Federal with Confederate—until such time as we no longer need each other."

"What can you offer us, Sergeant?" asked Sherrod.

"I want those women, and ye want those weapons. Neither of us gives a fiddler's damn what happens to Darris and his bloody crew, including Millard Artenis. Agreed?"

"Yes."

"Then I have a plan."

Ainsley grinned. "I knew it!"

Gallagher lowered his voice. "The moon will rise before long. Darris will be expecting you. Take me up there under guard and turn me over to him. Agree to everything he says."

"You're loco!" said Ainsley.

"Listen, dammit! I am not talking through me hat! There is a way into that western house that I don't think they know about. When I am inside those walls I will try to make my presence interesting enough so that the sentries will not be on the alert. Sergeant Gerry and Luke can take a party av picked men, the real boyos of yer command, and move up through yon trees and brush to a place near the pond.

"The spring water pours into the north end av the pond. The spring starts under the eastern house, runs through a tunnel under the courtyard, enters a stone trough in the end room av the western house, then out av the room into yon pond. Ye can enter the pool when the sentries are not looking, crawl into the house where the trough comes out, and be inside the westerly house."

Gallagher took a stick and sketched out the layout of the great house on the earth. "When ye move in ye must move fast! Once ye get yer hands on Darris and Artenis we might be able to dicker with the boys who are on guard up on the cliffs."

Gerry rubbed his lean jaw. "Sounds loco, but it might work."

"Ye have any better idea?" asked Gallagher sarcastically. "I tell ye it will work! It has to work!"

Sherrod nodded. "We'll go through with it."

Gallagher looked at Gerry and Ainsley. "Ye must leave enough men to move about these fires to make it look as though none of ye are missing."

The officer looked up at the canyon wall. "The moon is rising," he said quietly. He looked at Gallagher. "Whatever it is you plan to do inside those walls, I hope to God it works, or none of us will get out of this place alive."

Gallagher nodded. "One thing ye must all remember: Those men are good fighters and they will fight. Kill or be killed. *Deguelo.*"

"What do you mean by that?" asked Gerry.

"No quarter," said Gallagher. There was a hard look on his face.

The moon was touching the rim of the canyon when the rebel officer came to Gallagher. "Ready?" he quietly asked.

"As much as I'll ever be, sir."

"Come on then. Everything is ready."

They walked up the slope until a sentry on the wall called them to halt.

"I am here to see Darris," said the officer.

The two men stood in the moonlight waiting. In a little while the small door set in the gate was opened, and as they passed through they were examined for weapons. Sherrod was relieved of his pistol and knife.

Elijah Darris stood in the courtyard with his men about him, their faces as hard as glacial ice. Millard Artenis stood on the balcony porch of the eastern house looking down on the scene with a faint smile on his handsome face.

"Have you agreed to my terms?" asked Darris.

Sherrod nodded. "I have no other choice. I have written out an agreement to the effect that you and your people will not be bothered by my government. I have also written that payment, in gold, will be made for those weapons."

Darris half closed his eyes and glanced at Gallagher,

and the hairs on Gallagher's neck seemed to rise stiffly. Darris was too shrewd a fox to be taken in lightly.

"And where is the gold, may I ask?" said Darris.

Sherrod flushed. "I don't carry that much money with me," he said. "I have several thousand dollars in Confederate money, however, and I will turn that over to you, upon receipt of the weapons."

"Trash," said Darris contemptuously.

"What is that, suh?"

"I say your Confederate money is trash."

Sherrod started forward, then stayed himself as their weapons were raised. "What is it you want me to do then?" he asked in a strained voice.

Darris shrugged. "Klij-Litzogue promises me raw gold. It means nothing to them. They have no use for it. He promises me burro loads of the ore in exchange for the weapons."

The Confederate officer paled. "But you know what that means, suh! The Tontos will cut a bloody swath throughout Arizona with those weapons."

Darris smiled faintly. "And what did *you* expect to do with them, Captain?"

"He has ye there, Captain," said Gallagher out of the side of his mouth.

"Whether you obey the laws of the United States or the laws of the Confederate States of America does not matter, Darris," said Sherrod, "but there are greater laws. The unwritten laws of humanity. You cannot sell those weapons to the Tontos."

Darris walked slowly forward. "I will sell them to whom I please, soldier."

Sherrod looked up at Millard Artenis. "Can't you do anything about his attitude, Artenis?"

The man shook his head. He was watching Gallagher. "I don't give a tinker's damn for the Confederacy *or* the United States, Sherrod. I'm only interested in Sergeant Gallagher."

"Do tell," said Gallagher.

"It seems as though everyone wants a crack at you, Gallagher," said Artenis.

"I didn't know I was that popular," said Gallagher with a grin.

"I told you once that it was a pity that we two could not meet on the field of honor because of our social levels."

"Do tell."

Artenis casually flicked dust from the sleeves of his neat shell jacket. "But I have arranged something that will repay me for the beating you gave me at Fort McComber."

Gallagher raised his two fists. "Ye'll fight me, Artenis?" he said eagerly.

"No. But I have paid someone to fight for me. Someone to whom you also owe a debt."

The big barrel-chested man named Bart stepped forward, spat into both palms, and slapped his hands hard on his muscular thighs. "Me, you Irish son of a bitch," he said with a grin.

Hunter Sherrod looked at Darris. "This is foolishness," he said. "We have business to take care of."

Darris raised a hand. "It will be a pleasure to see this arrogant bragging swine beaten to a pulp before we throw his bloody body to the Tontos."

Sherrod stepped forward. Again the guns came up, but the Texan was not afraid. "This man is not in good condition," he said. "Look at him! You've done everything you can to break him."

Gallagher spat. "And failed," he said. He caught Sherrod's eye. The silent message sped between them. This was the chance; the opportunity for Gerry and Ainsley to get into the building.

"Get the women," said Darris thinly. "Let them see blood."

The moon was at such a height that it flooded the courtyard with light. Bart slowly stripped to the waist. His chest hair and beard looked even blacker in the moonlight against the white skin.

Gallagher peeled off his shirt and undershirt. The rude bandages that swathed his upper body were dirty and encrusted with dried blood. Gallagher stripped them off, wincing as the rough cloth tore loose from the scabs. Blood began to trickle from some of the deep welts.

THE BORDER GUIDON 145

"Good God!" said Sherrod. "Who did that, Gallagher?"

Gallagher turned slowly, and his face was a terrible thing to see in the pale moonlight. He jerked a thumb toward Bart. "Him," he said softly, almost gently, and the hidden menace in his voice struck home to Sherrod.

A door opened on the second-floor porch of the easterly building. Ellen and Judith Eustis came out and stood by the railing near Millard Artenis.

"Time," said Darris.

They advanced toward each other. Bart was heavy and meaty, and his muscles were thick and wide. There was a terrible power in him. Gallagher hoped to God he could stay on his feet until the Texans attacked.

Bart spat and reached out a toe to mark a line on the hard earth. Just as he did so a rock-hard fist caught him under the left ear and drove him back. "Damn you! It ain't time!" spluttered Bart.

Gallagher grinned. "Old whiskers said 'time' clearly enough, or would ye rather draw pictures on the ground?"

Bart rushed in, throwing hard short punches, and Gallagher was driven back as the blows battered at rib cage, face, and belly alternately. He bumped into Sherrod, and the officer shoved him back toward Bart. He sank a left into Bart's thick belly and measured him for a smashing right cross. The backs of Bart's legs struck the edge of a water trough and he sat down heavily.

Gallagher was upon him before he could get to his feet. He struck him viciously on the head two or three times, then gripped the man's thick hair and soused him under while the overflowing water soaked his own legs. He pulled up the dripping head. "Have ye had enough, *hombre!*" he roared into a wet ear.

Gallagher jumped backward as Bart kicked out. The big man struggled to his feet, but Gallagher hit him with a perfectly timed one-two that dumped him back over the trough.

Gallagher stepped back. He was tiring. He had drained too much stamina from his body in the past few days.

Bart got up slowly, water dripping from his clothing and forming little puddles beside his big feet. He rounded the trough, pure hell on his face. He plunged toward Gallagher with short little steps, swinging both arms in vicious hooks.

"*Now,* Bart!" yelled Artenis.

It was as though he was chopping wood with short smashing blows of the ax, and when he was done Gallagher lay sprawled on the ground with blood running brightly in the moonlight from nose and mouth. His brain reeled sickeningly. He was licked. God how he was licked!

Bart straddled Gallagher. He moved slowly, reaching with big bloody hands for Gallagher's face, while the stubby powerful thumbs felt for the eyeballs. Darris laughed. "Let him go blind to his maker," he said.

"Gallagher!" screamed Ellen. "The guidon! The Border Guidon! It must go back to the regiment!"

Her words called forth Gallagher's last reserves. He twisted his head free from the terrible hands and bent it forward, then drove it up with all his strength into Bart's groin. The man grunted in sudden agony. Gallagher got to his feet. Bart charged right into a fist that Gallagher held out in front of him. Bart reeled, and he was helped in his downfall by a right-handed crusher that drove his beak of a nose up half an inch. His head cracked dully against a porch post on the way down. Gallagher booted him. It was a mistake, for Bart gripped the leg and upended Gallagher. The two of them thrashed over and over across the hard earth of the courtyard until they were almost at the feet of Darris.

Then they were up on their feet with science thrown to the night wind. It was hit, knee, gouge, and bite—and never let up, for if you did you would no longer resemble a man.

They broke free at last and staggered away from each other, blood running from their faces to form little black pools on the moon-silvered earth.

Their eyes were wide in their heads, but they did not hesitate to close in again. Bart drove Gallagher back. Gallagher covered up and kept retreating, but his legs were fast weakening, and they shook with the strain of

THE BORDER GUIDON

him staying on his feet. He was almost beaten by this bearded rock of a man. Then, beyond the sweating hairy shoulders of Bart, he saw the end door of the western building open a little. Ainsley and Gerry! It had to be!

Gallagher drew upon an unknown source of power and threw it into the scales. Blood flew from the battered face of the big man as he slowly retreated. Sergeant Gerry was out in the open now, running lightly toward Darris with a pistol in his hand. Then Ainsley was out in the courtyard followed by dripping Texans. Someone cursed to break the spell. A carbine cracked, and a Texan died. Gun shots crackled out through a weaving shifting veil of smoke. A man raised a rifle to shoot at Gallagher, but Captain Sherrod snatched up an iron bucket and threw it hard and straight to drop the rifleman.

Bart reached down and snatched up a length of heavy wagon chain. He whirled it over his head like a terrible flail and advanced on Gallagher as the shooting crackled fiercely from both sides and echoed back and forth between the walls of the two buildings. Sherrod ran to the south gate and threw the bar to the ground, then pulled open the gate. The rest of Company G poured in.

As the chain clipped Gallagher on the forearm he screamed like a woman. He darted behind a post, and the chain wound viciously around it. Gallagher kicked Bart in the groin, then followed up with the last punch he had in the locker, snapping it up under the thick beard. Bart's head struck the stone wall. There was the sound of a dropped melon, and Bart dropped sideways. His eyes were wide in his head, but he did not see. He would never see again.

Darris yelled in a mad frenzy as he darted in through a lower door in the east building. Gallagher looked up toward the women. They stood there together, frozen. Millard Artenis was running toward the north wall of the courtyard. Gallagher raced for the stairs and caught the heel of a boot on his chin. Then Artenis placed a hand on the wall and vaulted cleanly to land on the hard earth below. By the time Gallagher got to the top of the stairs the man was gone.

Gallagher thought of Darris. He burst a door open with a shoulder and looked through one room after another until he found the man. The man was on his knees. Tears streamed down his face and trickled into his beard. "Don't punish me!" he screamed.

Gallagher spat. He twisted a hand in the heavy beard and dragged Darris after him, bumping him cruelly down the stairs to the smoke-filled courtyard. The fight was over. The Texans stood around grinning. "Two dead, three wounded, suh," reported Sergeant Gerry. The grins vanished.

"And the others?" asked Sherrod.

Gerry turned with an odd look on his face. "*Deguelo,*" he said. "No Quarter." He jerked a thumb at Darris. "Just him, suh." The sergeant cocked his pistol.

Hunter Sherrod wiped the sweat from his face. "Thanks, Gallagher. Without you we could never have managed it. But for a time there I thought he surely had you . . . until the woman called out."

Gallagher wiped the blood from his face with his free hand. "Aye," he said quietly, "it was a near thing, that."

"The rest of them are coming down the trail, suh!" yelled a corporal. "Do we open fire?"

There was a strange look on Sherrod's face. "We take only the women from this hellhole," he said clearly.

So it was. Texans have a habit of shooting straight. They waste no ammunition. When the last echo of the battle died away down the canyon the only man left alive outside of Millard Artenis was Elijah Darris, the old devil himself, and the madness that had always hovered behind his icy eyes had full control now.

Chapter 18

THE Texans were piling food and stores together beside the buildings. Horses and mules had been rounded up to carry the supplies and weapons from the cliff dwellings. Luke Ainsley had slipped down the canyon to scout the Apaches. Sergeant Gerry had sent a detail to bring down enough Sharps carbines and Colt revolving pistols to arm the company adequately. The troopers grinned as they handled the fine weapons. "Sure kin go through them Yankees west of heah like crap through a tin horn," said a big corporal.

"Where's Gallagher?" asked Captain Sherrod.

"Went to get his hoss and his damned old Yankee guidon, suh."

"Won't do him any good hauling that guidon to a prison," said Sergeant Gerry.

Ellen Eustis stood close to the wall watching the troopers. Judith sat on a chair some distance from her sister. They did not speak to each other. There was a coldness between them that would never be replaced with the warmth of sisterly love.

Hunter Sherrod looked toward the corrals. "Gallagher has been gone a long time," he said suddenly.

"He wanted to bathe," said Ellen.

The officer nodded. He eyed her appreciatively. No wonder Gallagher had fought so hard. She was a beauty. A thoroughbred. The other one? Well, she was a beauty, too, in a different sort of a way. A man knew where she was headed. "I don't know how we can get you two ladies through the Apache lines," he said quietly.

"I can shoot," said Ellen.

The moon was on the wane now. Gallagher came up the slope from the stream. "What now, Captain?" he asked.

"We'll have to break through. The Confederacy needs these weapons. We'll lose men, but we came here for weapons, and we must pay a price for them."

"Not a chance," said Gallagher. "Ye do not know Yellow Snake. He'll not fight ye in the open, but will use the swift ambush when ye least expect it. He'll cut down yer men one by one."

"I have no recourse but to try and break through."

Ainsley came up the slope. "They're still there," he said quietly. "They've picked out two positions, one on each side of the canyon, and they can cover every inch of the bare ground between them with rifle fire. We can't get out that way, sir."

"There is no other way," said Gallagher, "not for ye and yer heavily laden horses and mules. Even if ye did get part of yer command past them they'd cut ye down in the desert country."

Hunter Sherrod slapped his gauntlets against his thigh. Indecision was written across his tired face.

"I'll make a deal with ye, sir," said Gallagher.

"Go on, Sergeant."

"I do not want to go to a ribil prison, sir. If I get ye past the Tontos will ye free me and the lasses with horses, weapons, and supplies?"

"How can you get us through?"

Gallagher smiled slyly. "First, the word of an officer and a gentleman, which I know ye to be, sir."

"On my honor, Gallagher."

Gallagher grinned. "There are some brass mountain howitzers up there, sir. I can show ye a place to set one av them up not far from the mouth av the canyon. When the time comes for ye to make yer break the howitzer can be fired into the Tonto ambush. I have yet to see Indians who would stand up to well-served artillery."

The officer eyed him. "But the men who stay behind to serve the gun will surely be lost."

Gallagher grinned again and cocked an eye. "I did some time in the artillery when I was a recruitie. The gun can be placed within the taboo limits av the canyon. They will not try to rush it."

"You'll need help."

Ellen came forward. "Gallagher can teach me," she said.

There was stark admiration in Sherrod's eyes. "Damme, what a woman! Begging your pardon, ma'am!"

Judith swaggered up to them. "Don't count me in," she sneered. "I'm not going with *them*."

"What do you mean?" demanded Sherrod.

She looked archly at Sergeant Gerry, who turned away with reddening face. "I think I'd prefer living under the Stars and Bars rather than the Stars and Stripes. Is there any objection?"

"None," he said quietly.

Gallagher saluted the officer. "And now, if the captain is ready let us get the gun and move it into position."

"But the other howitzers?" said Sherrod wearily.

Gallagher shrugged. "Ye cannot get them out of the canyon, sir."

"No." Sherrod smiled. "But neither can the Federals."

The horses and mules were laden with the supplies. Box after box after box of Sharps carbines, Colt revolving pistols, ammunition and caps, followed by one of the stubby brass howitzers. Gallagher checked its accessories—powder charges, shells, friction tubes and lanyard, rammer, and wads. "Artillery section all correct sir," he said to Sherrod.

"No chance of you joining the 'ribils' is there, Gallagher?"

"None, sir."

Sherrod indicated the laden mules and horses. "That equipment will sway the balance in our favor in this territory, Sergeant. I'm sorry that you will end up on the losing side."

Gallagher shook his head in mock sadness. "I have me loyalty to think of first, sir, win or lose."

Sherrod flushed. "Move out!" he commanded.

Gallagher followed the troopers and the mule train with his gun being hauled by two mules. Behind the gun rode Ellen on big Shannon, leading another horse and a laden pack mule. She had bound her hair with a yellow ribbon. "Cavalry colors," Gallagher had said sadly as he led out his section.

The false dawn lightened the eastern sky. Sweating Texans had silently hauled the gun up the western wall of the canyon to a wide rock shelf that overlooked the canyon mouth. Gallagher fiddled with the elevating screw for a time, then blew a breath upon the fat breech of the gun and solicitously polished it with a very dirty sleeve.

Ellen sat on a rock beside the gun with the rammer across her lap and the wads, shells, and powder charges piled neatly beside her.

It grew lighter. Sherrod had said he would charge after the first shot from the howitzer. The sky was tinted with rich gold. Gallagher placed a friction tube in the vent of the loaded gun and attached the lanyard to it. "Ye will remember what to do?" he asked her.

"Yes."

"Yes, what!"

"Yes, Sergeant!" She smiled thinly. "Now, Sergeant?"

"Now," he said as he stepped to one side and gave the lanyard a hard clean pull. The little gun roared valiantly and rammed back in recoil. The smoke blew out in a perfect ring, and the shell burst in a red-orange blossom shrouded in thick white smoke right in the center of one of the Tonto positions.

Gallagher heaved the gun back into position and thumbed the vent. "Sponge!" he snapped.

She moved like a veteran redleg, plunging the sponge end of the rammer into the water bucket, driving it into the smoking muzzle of the gun, then withdrawing it, steaming blackly.

"Load!"

Powder charge and wad went in and were rammed home with a thud by the brass end of the rammer staff. The shell followed, with another wad behind it. Gallagher placed the friction tube and attached the lanyard. "Stand clear!" he roared and jerked the lanyard. The gun spat

THE BORDER GUIDON 153

flame and smoke. Far below them they could hear the thrilling piercing yell of the Texans as they charged.

The thunder of pounding hoofs filled the canyon with sound. Hand guns sparkled death in the growing light as Captain Hunter Sherrod led G Company, Sixth Texas Mounted Rifles, through the gap, while a redheaded Irish dragoon and a raven-haired girl worked as a gun team that sowed red fire blossoms in the Tonto positions, spewing hot metal and sudden death through the chapparral. The dry brush flared up, and in a few minutes the fresh wind was fanning the flames higher and higher. The yelling Texans burst through the thick wall of smoke and were in the clear, with the pack mules thudding along behind them, braying in terror.

The last shot from the howitzer struck just behind a running warrior, lifting him upward with arms and legs splayed out like a human sacrifice, and before he struck the ground Gallagher knew Klij-Litzogue was on the way to the House of Spirits.

Gallagher neatly spiked the little gun and heaved it over the side of the cliff. It bounced and crashed its way to the rocky bottom.

"Come on, lass," said Gallagher as he wiped the sweat from his battered face.

They walked down the trail to where they had left the horses and the mule. Ellen looked through the rifted smoke to the thread of dust rising from the hoofs of the Texans' animals. "Those weapons might win the war for them, Gallagher," she said.

"Aye, they *might*. . ."

"You don't seem concerned, Gallagher! This isn't like you!"

"There is no time to waste talking! Mount!"

"I'm not a dragoon!"

He drew his fingers across his tattered faded stripes and diamond. "Ye see these? I'm the first soldier here and don't ye forget it!"

"How can I?" she retorted. But she mounted quickly enough to follow him through the thick brush. The faded guidon snapped in the fresh breeze.

The sun was well up when they reached the deserted buildings. "Look!" said Ellen suddenly.

A naked figure danced about one of the roofs, his beard waving in the wind. Thin, maniacal laughter echoed from the canyon walls.

"Darris," said Gallagher. He shivered.

They could still hear his laughter as they spurred through the quiet woods.

They did not see Millard Artenis until they had cleared the woods. He stood in the trail with a cocked pistol in his right hand. They drew rein. "Well, Gallagher?" said the ex-officer.

Gallagher eyed the man. "Get out of the way. Yer Texan friends are gone. The United States will not have ye. Where will ye go, Artenis?"

The man's face worked. "I'll get out of here," he said.

"Past the Tontos?"

The color drained from his face. "Damn you, Gallagher! At least I can finish *you* off!" He raised the pistol. Something cracked deafeningly alongside Gallagher's head, and stinking powder smoke swirled past his face. Through the smoke Gallagher could see Artenis gripping his right wrist with his left hand while the gun dropped from nerveless fingers. Blood leaked between the fingers of his left hand. He stared at the girl.

Ellen lowered her smoking pistol. "Let's go home, Gallagher," she said quietly.

They rode past the white-faced man. He opened his mouth. "But what about me?" he shrieked.

Gallagher grinned. "Yes," he said. "What about ye? Go back to the buildings, *Mister* Artenis, ye'll have good company there."

They rode on, never looking back.

It was middle afternoon when Gallagher found the dim trail that would lead them from the canyon to the trail to Fort Yuma. They stopped to rest the animals. The big pack mule was very tired.

Ellen lay back and looked at the bright sky, shading her lovely eyes with her hands. "Those guns," she said quietly. "In a few months I expect to hear that the rebels have conquered the territory—and perhaps the Pacific Coast—with them, Gallagher."

"Aye," he said.

"You puzzle me! Wasn't there something we could have done?"

"Aye."

"What?"

He walked to the mule and stripped two heavy bags from it. They clinked as he lowered them to the ground. He opened one of the bags and took out a metal object which he showed to her.

"What is it? What do you have in those bags?"

He whistled softly. "Breechblocks from Sharps carbines and cylinders from Colt revolving pistols, lass. It seems as though Gallagher was a very busy boyo up in those dwellings whilst the trusting Texans were down below thinking only of supplies for their bellies. Sure, they have the fine weapons, but without these breechblocks and cylinders they will be of no use, and ye cannot frighten the mean Yankee soldiers with such weapons, can ye now?"

She roared with laughter. "Now I know why you were gone bathing so long and still did not smell like a rose when you came back with grease on your fingers!"

He nodded. "Poor Captain Sherrod. A hero he will be until the giniral finds he has brought back useless weapons for the all-important campaign. And, to me knowledge, the only spare breechblocks and cylinders in the whole Southwest are in the hands of the Yankees, and they won't part with 'em, lass."

He carried the bags to the stream and dumped them in a deep hole. He stared down into the water, then walked upstream a little way to a riffle. Then suddenly he waded in and scooped up some of the sand. It glittered in his big hand. He walked back to her and placed the sand in her hands. "Gold," he said quietly. "The stream is full of it."

She looked up at him. "What good is it to us, Gallagher?"

He looked up the bright canyon at the soft waving

trees and the flashing stream laden with yellow riches. "The war will not last forever," he said at last. "A man could come here and make a fine home."

"But it is haunted," she said. "Darris and Artenis."

"They will hunt each other down and they will die, one way or another. Or, if they are still here when I come back I will hunt them down meself."

She shivered a little. "If a person lived here they would still be haunted of nights by those two men, Gallagher."

He smiled. "There is one thing that can drive them away, if their spirits haunt this place."

"So? What is it?"

He bent and kissed her gently. "The laughter of little children, lass," he answered. "Nature will cleanse this place. It always does."

She got to her feet and walked to her horse. She fumbled with her hair. "Gallagher!" she called out.

He walked to her.

"Tie up my hair," she said. She handed him an orange ribbon.

The guidon snapped in the breeze as they rode toward the trail. She looked up at it. "The Border Guidon," she said. "It knows it is going home to the regiment."

They rode up the trail side by side. The last United States soldier in Arizona Territory was leaving. But he'd be back before too long, and he would not come alone. He and his comrades would follow the Border Guidon back to where it belonged—on the fighting border between the United States and its enemies, whoever they might be.

Other SIGNET Westerns You'll Enjoy

☐ **RIDE THE WILD TRAIL by Cliff Farrell.** Steve Santee returned to Powderhorn Basin to clear his father's name, and found himself marked for murder. . . .
(#Q6221—95¢)

☐ **COMANCH by Cliff Farrell.** They called him 'Comanch', the Indian, with contempt . . . but was he an Indian?
(#Q6104—95¢)

☐ **PATCHSADDLE DRIVE by Cliff Farrell.** Trail boss Clay Burnet was saddled with a ragtag crew, a furious feud, and a bloody quest for vengeance! (#T5706—75¢)

☐ **THE SCORPION KILLERS by Ray Hogan.** Was the mysterious Amigo his long-lost brother? A posse dogs his heels as Shawn Starbuck tries to find out!
(#T5941—75¢)

☐ **THE MARSHAL by Frank Gruber.** He'd sworn to uphold the peace, but the town made him a killer!
(#Q5987—95¢)

☐ **THE TOMBSTONE TRAIL by Ray Hogan.** Shawn Starbuck encounters a girl named Glory, owner of a silver mine thieves were determined to plunder!
(#Q6070—95¢)

THE NEW AMERICAN LIBRARY, INC.,
P.O. Box 999, Bergenfield, New Jersey 07621

Please send me the SIGNET BOOKS I have checked above. I am enclosing $_____(check or money order—no currency or C.O.D.'s). Please include the list price plus 25¢ a copy to cover handling and mailing costs. (Prices and numbers are subject to change without notice.)

Name_____

Address_____

City_____State_____Zip Code_____

Allow at least 3 weeks for delivery

Still More Westerns from SIGNET

- [ ] **RETURN OF THE LONG RIDERS by Cliff Farrell.** A tragic feud turned friendship into hate, violence, and murder!
(#Q6323—95¢)

- [ ] **THE ORPHANS OF COYOTE CREEK by Lewis B. Patten.** Three spunky kids fight off a vicious killer in this new novel of the West by the Spur award-winning bestselling author. (#Q6322—95¢)

- [ ] **THE BUSHWHACKERS by Frank Gruber.** The thunderbolt novel of an innocent man accused of riding with Quantrell's raiders in a reign of terror and massacre.
(#Q6263—95¢)

- [ ] **TROUBLE SHOOTER by Ernest Haycox.** The lusty, roaring novel about Frank Peace and his relentless battle to get the railroad through. (#Q6262—95¢)

- [ ] **THE TEXAS BRIGADE by Ray Hogan.** Joining a strange posse tracking a wagon train kidnapped by Comancheros, Starbuck is trapped in a last-ditch stand. . . .
(#Q6154—95¢)

- [ ] **SHOOTOUT AT SIOUX WELLS by Cliff Farrell.** When tough cattleman Zack Keech became undercover agent for the railroad he despised, violence was bound to erupt! (#Q5911—95¢)

THE NEW AMERICAN LIBRARY, INC.,
P.O. Box 999, Bergenfield, New Jersey 07621

Please send me the SIGNET BOOKS I have checked above. I am enclosing $_____(check or money order—no currency or C.O.D.'s). Please include the list price plus 25¢ a copy to cover handling and mailing costs. (Prices and numbers are subject to change without notice.)

Name_____

Address_____

City_____State_____Zip Code_____
Allow at least 3 weeks for delivery

HANDY FILES AND CASES FOR STORING MAGAZINES, CASSETTES, & 8-TRACK CARTRIDGES

CASSETTE STORAGE CASES
Decorative cases, custom-made of heavy bookbinder's board, bound in Kid-Grain Leatherette, a gold-embossed design. Individual storage slots slightly tilted back to prevent handling spillage. Choice of: Black, brown, green.

#JC-30—30 unit size (13½x5½x6½") $11.95 ea.
3 for $33.00

#JC-60—60 unit size (13½x5½x12⅝") $16.95 ea.
3 for $48.00

MAGAZINE VOLUME FILES
Keep your favorite magazines in mint condition. Heavy bookbinder's board is covered with scuff-resistant Kivar. Specify the title of the magazine and we'll send the right size case. If the title is well-known it will appear on the spine in gold letters. For society journals, a brass-rimmed window is attached and gold foil included—you type the title.

#J-MV—Magazine Volume Files $4.95 ea.
3 for $14.00
6 for $24.00

8-TRACK CARTRIDGE STORAGE CASE
This attractive unit measures 13¾ inches high, 6½ inches deep, 4½ inches wide, has individual storage slots for 12 cartridges and is of the same sturdy construction and decorative appearance as the Cassette Case.

#J-8T12—4½" wide (holds 12 cartridges)
$8.50 ea.
3 for $23.50

#J-8T24—8½" wide (holds 24 cartridges)
$10.95 ea.
3 for $28.00

#J-8T36—12¾" wide (holds 36 cartridges)
$14.25 ea.
3 for $37.00

Please send:

ITEM NO	COLOR (IF CHOICE)	DESCRIPTION	QUANTITY	UNIT PRICE	TOTAL COST

Postage and handling charges (up to $10 add $1.50) ($10.01 to $20 add $2.50) ($20.01 to $40 add $3.50)
(over $40 postage FREE)
I enclose ☐ check ☐ money order in amount of $ _____ Total _____

The New American Library, Inc.
P.O. Box 999
Bergenfield, New Jersey 07621

Name _____
Address _____
City _____ State _____ Zip _____

Offer valid only in the United States of America.   (Allow 5 weeks for delivery.)

HI-RISE BOOK CASES
THE ANSWER TO YOUR
PAPER BACK BOOK
STORAGE PROBLEM

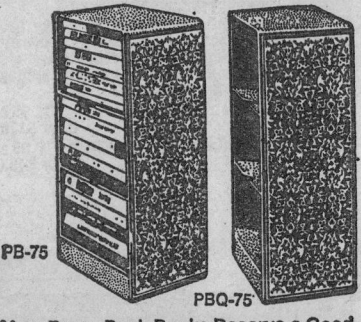

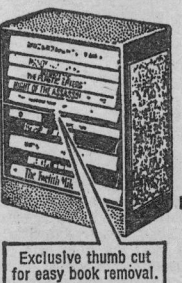

PB-75

PBQ-75

PB-71

Exclusive thumb cut for easy book removal.

Your Paper Back Books Deserve a Good Home Free From Dust, Dirt and Dogears.

Save shelf space; keep paper back books attractively stored, dust-proof, readily accessible.

- All-new Storage Case with handsome, padded leatherette covering complements any room decor, stores approximately 15 books compactly, attractively.
- Shelves tilted back to prevent books from falling out.
- Handsome outer case elegantly embossed in gold leaf—choice of 4 decorator colors: black, brown, green, red.
- Gold transfer foil slip enclosed for quick 'n easy personalization.

PB-75. Stores app. 15 books compactly, attractively. 13¼" H x 8" D x 4¾" W. **$7.95 EA.** 2/$15.00 3/$22.00

PB-71. For smaller shelves. Holds app. 11 books. 9¼" H x 8" D x 4¾" W. **$6.50 EA.** 2/$12.75 3/$18.75

PBQ-75. Stores app. 15 books compactly, attractively. 13¼" H x 8½" D x 5½" W. OVERSIZE **$9.50 EA.** 2/$18.50 3/$27.00

The New American Library, Inc.
P.O. Box 999, Bergenfield, New Jersey 07621

(quant.) (color)

Please send _____ PB-75 _____ @ $ _____

_____ PB-71 _____ @ $ _____

_____ PBQ-75 _____ @ $ _____

Postage and handling charges (up to $10, add $1.50) ($10.01-$20, add $2.50) ($20.01-$40, add $3.50) (over $40, post. FREE)

I enclose ☐ check ☐ money order in amount of $ _____

Name _____

Address _____

City _____ State _____ Zip _____

(Allow 5 weeks for delivery.) Offer valid only in the United States of America.